CAPTAIN GAULT

CAPTAIN GAULT

BEING THE EXCEEDINGLY
PRIVATE LOG OF A SEA-CAPTAIN

WILLIAM HOPE HODGSON

1918

CONTENTS

CAPTAIN GAULT

CHAPTER I

MY LADY'S JEWELS

s.s. *London City,*
March 4.

Women have a great trick of asking me to help them through the Customs with their jewelry.

I've said "Yes" once or twice, and not always had occasion to regret it. You see, there are women who are more honest than you'd think a woman could be, considering just what a woman is.

I make it a general rule, though, to say "No" to these requests, for it's bad policy to mix up business and pleasure; and I've no use for a woman when it comes to sharing a secret with her. She's so apt to be a bit mixed in her ideas of fair play.

It's all rot to say a woman can't keep a secret. She can! She could keep a secret till Old Nick turned gray, begging for it, *if it suited her.* But that's just the trouble! You never know when it's going to stop suiting her to keep mum. If she gets the notion there's more cash for her in talk, than in keeping quiet, she'll pull the lid off and let the secret pop out, regardless of the hole you may get shoved into as a result.

Anyway, I can't help making friends occasionally on the trip across. And there's a Mrs. Ernley, a pretty young widow, American, with heaps of dollars, who's shown a friendly side to me since the first day out.

I spotted her the moment she came aboard, and I gave the Chief Steward word to put her at my table. There are always little compensations, like that, to make up for the long hours, short pay, and big responsibilities of a sea-captain's life!

We got on splendidly; and as she had no one to look after her, I have done my best ever since.

She was up with me on the lower bridge to-day, helping me "keep the watch," she called it; though it's not much watch I can keep when she's looking up at me, and saying things, of an "Americanness" beyond belief, and of an artlessness that ought to be beyond propriety, but somehow isn't.

"I've bought a heap of stuff in London and Paris," she told me; "and I'm afraid the New York Customs will sure have it in savage for me, Captain Gault."

"I'm afraid so," I said.

I was truly afraid; for that's the way a lot of them lead up to asking me to help them hide the stuff somewhere in the ship, so as to get it safely past the Customs searchers.

"It's a mighty wicked tax," she said. "I wish we women had the vote, we'd alter things. I s'pose you don't think a woman's fit to vote, Captain. But let me tell you, she's a heap fitter than half the men."

"I'm not against the vote," I said, "under conditions that are fair to the men."

"What's fair to one is fair to the other!" she said.

"That's a bit vague," I told her. "The suffrage is largely the modern equivalent of physical force. Women have less of it by nature, than men, and consequently there is a certain artificiality in the situation of a woman voting on equal terms with a man; for it implies that she is *physically* the equal of the man."

"Might's not right!" she said, warmly. "A clever woman has more brains than a laborer. Yet you give *him* the vote!"

"Exactly!" I said, smiling a little at her feminine method of meeting my distinctly masculine argument. "The laboring man has the vote, when you haven't it, because the vote is the modern equivalent of *physical* strength. Nowadays, when a man wants a things, he votes for it, instead of fighting for it. In the old days, he fought for it, and would to-day, if his vote were outvoted by a lot of people who were *physically* midgets. The vote is might as well as right. All the same, ethically, the very cows in the fields have a right to vote. I wonder how they'd vote on the pure butter question, and the vealing of their calves!"

"I'm not interested one bit about cows having the vote," she said; "but I tell you, Captain, when we women get the vote, we'll wipe this wicked tax on women's jewelry, and pretty things, clean off the slate! If things go on like this, only very rich women will be able to dress at all."

"I hadn't thought of it in that light," I said. "How shocking! Still there's always the cheaper sorts of dress stuffs—plain cotton prints can look quite pretty. No need really, you know, to allow this man-made tax to achieve its abominable end——"

"Captain," she interrupted, suddenly, "will you do something for me?"

I knew then that I could not delay the fatal moment any longer. She was going to ask me to risk liberty and profession for the sake of her pocket. And being a man, what chance had I?

"Captain Gault," she said, "I bought something enormously expensive when I was in Paris."

"Yes," I asked, rather hopelessly, "was it a necklace or a tiara?"

"Look!" she said, and opened her handbag.

"What did you pay for that?" I asked. "You ought to have it locked up in the strong room. For goodness' sake, don't let any one aboard know you've got a thing like that with you. A sea-captain's responsibilities are bad enough, without adding to them gratuitously. Do shut the bag, please, and take it to the strong room! It'll be much safer there."

"I paid nearly a million dollars for it," she said, looking up at me; "and I guess that's as much as I'm going to pay. I'm going to smuggle it through the Customs. I'm not going·to pay a cent of their horrible wicked tax."

"Mrs. Ernley," I said, "it's evident you don't know much about the U.S.A. Customs people. Let me tell you, dear lady, they're smart; and the chances are they know at the present moment that you've bought this necklace, and what you've paid for it."

"No," she said, "they don't just know anything at all about it, Captain. I made up my mind that I wouldn't pay the tax. Why, it would be about six hundred thousand dollars on this one necklace! It's just robbery! And so I made arrangements secretly through a friend, with Monsieur Jervoyn, the jeweller, to meet me at her house, and I bought this lovely thing there, and paid for it in cash. So you see, they *can't* know!"

"My dear Mrs. Ernley," I remonstrated,
"never be sure of anything where the U.S.A.
Customs are concerned, except that they're
on the job all the time. Americans are like
that, as you know. If they go in for graft,
they do the thing properly; and if they go in
for doing their duty, they do it properly
likewise, in about forty different ways at one
and the same time. That's the way they're
built. They've got to be efficient per lb. whatever else they are or are not. And you can
bet on this, when the Customs come aboard
in New York, they'll know you've got this,
and they'll know the name of the man you got
it from; and they'll be able to make a shot at
what you paid for it."

She shook her head, obstinately. It's a
confoundedly pretty little head, and I don't
mind whether she shakes it or just nods. It
looks nice any way.

"I'm sure they don't know!" she asserted.
"I was far, far too careful. I was, now,
Captain; and I bet my last dollar they don't
even dream I've bought anything much. Not
for all their secret agents and things. Oh,
I know more of their ways than you think,

Captain Gault! I've heard some of my relations talk; and they're in the Treasury, and I know I'm up against something; but I guess I'll get the thing through all right, if you'll help me. You see, I've got it all plotted out, as clever as you like. I've got a proper plan. Will you help me, Captain? Oh, I don't mean that you're to risk things for nothing. I wouldn't have that! I'll pay you a percentage, if you will help me. . . . A percentage on what I paid for it, will you now?"

"Well," I said, after pausing a moment to think, "I might; but I don't like mixing business and friendship. I'm not set on having a percentage."

"That's the only way I'll deal with you, Captain Gault," she told me. "How would five or ten per cent. suit you?"

"Oh," I said, smiling a little at her casualness, "I guess two and a half per cent. will suit me very well indeed."

"That's settled, then," she replied. "Now, here's my plan. When I ordered the necklace, I stipulated that they should make me another —an exact facsimile of it, Carn glass—you

know that new glass stuff that looks as good
as the best paste?"

"Carn Prism glass, you mean?" I suggested.

She nodded.

"Yes, that's it," she said. "Well now,
I've the two here in my bag, and I can't tell
the difference, and wouldn't be able to, Captain, only I've tied a bit of silk round the
real one. Now this is my plan, you are to
take and hide the real one for me—oh, I
know you're a wonderful man at getting
things past the Customs! And I shall have
the false one in my bag. Then, *if* they've
got scent that I've bought a necklace, and
search me, they'll find the false one; and
they'll reckon they've been misinformed.
Then, after I'm searched, you can give me
back the real one as soon as things are safe,
and I'll give you a cheque for the five per
cent."

"Two and a half," I corrected her.

"Take me somewhere where I can give
you the thing," she went on, unheeding my
correction, and I took her into my chart-
room. Here she lifted the two necklaces

out of her bag. They were certainly wonderful; and though I could tell one from
the other, after an examination, they would
easily have deceived lots of men who think
they know diamonds "at sight"; and certainly, apart, I should have been puzzled to
say which was which, without making a
test.

"Very well," I said. "I'll hide it for
you in a safe place."

And with that she handed me the real
necklace—a regular chain of light—a mar-
vellous thing it is. And I put it away; but
refused to let her know how I should hide it.

March 6. Evening.

Women are as much like little girls as men
are like little boys, when it comes to jewelry. Mrs. Ernley coaxes me at least twice
a day to let her see and play with her gorgeous necklace. And while she plays with
it, sitting on the settee, in my chart-room, I
sit across on the locker and look at her.
She's a remarkably pretty woman!

"Why do you stare so at me, Captain
Gault?" she asked, this afternoon, looking

across at me, with a touch of pure mischief.

"I guess it's for the same reason you suppose it is, dear lady," I said, smiling a little at her pretence. "You're good to look at, and you're generally an interesting study for a man of my temperament. I'm wondering what next *trait* will come out in you —weakness or virtue. Frankly, I suspect weakness."

"Don't you make any error, Captain; there's no weakness about me!" she assured me, in her quaint way. "You can sure take that for a conviction!"

"A conviction, dear lady, should be that which is produced by the action of Reason upon Experience!" I told her. "Now my experience of you tells me that you are quite averagely human—a good average mixture of strengths and weaknesses. Up to the present, you've shown me your strong side. Now, Reason, acting upon Experience, bids me to expect the other side of the shield."

"Captain Gault!" she said, "you're going too deep for me. Now be sensible, and look at my shining beauty. Did you ever see the like now? I just had to buy it. I couldn't

say no. I'd like to see the woman that could.
You'll call that a weakness, I suppose!"

"A weakness that I'm not going to quarrel
with, seeing that it's going to put twenty-
five thousand dollars into my pocket," I told
her.

She looked so startled, that I had to
explain.

"That's my share, you know. Two and a
half per cent. on a million dollars is twenty-
five thousand."

"Oh!" she said, in rather a queer tone.
"Yes, of course. I never thought to work it
out."

I said nothing; but I could not help wondering whether it was here that the little
weakness was going to show up. It was obvious that she'd had a shock, when I explained to her just how much my commission
was going to cost her; though, goodness
knows, it's cheap enough, when one remem-
bers what the Customs would have rooked
her of. But you never know how women
are going to look at things of this kind.
Women are extraordinary mixtures of big
extravagances and petty economies.

She was pretty silent for the rest of the time she was in the chart-room; and I rallied her mildly on her sudden soberness.

"Dear lady," I said, "if the size of my fee troubleth thee (forgive the *tutoiement*), why I'll e'en hoodwink our common enemy for no more than the joy of the game and good friendship!"

She protested so hotly that this could not be thought of, and had so much good colour in her cheeks, that I had very little doubt but that I had shot true. However, she made it very clear indeed that my fee was mine, and that her word was more truly her bond than if it had been signed and stamped and sealed and lawyered. And all the time, she fiddled with the great, million-dollar chain-of-light, running it through and through her hands.

Then she handed it back to me, and went away to dress for dinner. And see the nature of woman! She had changed the necklaces. She had left with me the imitation, as I knew in a minute, by testing it. And, that it was no accident, I had easy proof; for she had shifted the mark (the piece of silk) from the real necklace to the imitation one.

Truly, it takes some twisting to follow a woman! But there is, in a matter of money, a simple rule to aid a man with a woman, if he would get at the truth of her motive. For, either her action is prompted by insane generosity or an even more insane meanness. And here it was not difficult to see what had governed her action. She had been shocked to see that out of a million dollars she had pledged herself to pay twenty-five thousand; and she had palmed me the false necklace, meaning to try to run the real one through herself, after all, and so avoid paying me my fee. She had lacked the moral courage to tell me so, honestly; but I suppose, once she is safe through the Customs with the real necklace, she will write me a polite little note, telling me that she decided to run the thing through herself. She may even ask me to keep the glass one as a souvenir; and, being a woman, she will not mean to be cynical. She will really wish me to accept it, in memory of her! Little wonder the simple, straightforward, logical male feels at sea; for a woman obeys her

impulses, while, all the time, he supposes
her to be using her reasoning powers, which,
by the way, are generally atrophied.

And now I'm interested to follow her
further manœuvres!

March 9.

"For the last couple of days you've not
asked to see your necklace," I told her, this
morning, after I had invited her up on to the
lower bridge. "And you're getting tired of
keeping the old sea-dog company! Confess
now, aren't you?"

"No," she answered. "I'm just denying
myself. I'm showing you I can be stronger
than you think."

"All women are liars," I whispered sol-
emnly, to myself. "I suppose they can't
help it, any more than a man can stop being
logical at some one else's expense."

But I said nothing out loud; and for a
minute or two, we walked the length of the
bridge, without saying a word.

"Being strong isn't just being strong in
the way you find easy to be strong," I said
at last.

"That sounds rather difficult," she answered. "Try now if you can't do some better than that, Captain Gault, or I'll miss what you want to tell me."

"I mean," I said, "that if I set out, say, not to tell lies, just to prove how much of a moral athlete I was, it would not prove anything; for the simple reason that lying is not my particular poison. Of course, if I've got to, I do it in a finished kind of fashion; but I've no particular Ananias leanings. Given two ways out of a difficulty, I'd not necessarily choose the lie. Sumga?"

"Sure I do," she said; "but I don't see what that's to do with my refraining from coming to see my nec—you and my necklace, I mean. I wanted badly to see both of you. No, don't get conceited! But I have kept away. Doesn't that show strength, to keep away from doing things you're wanting bad to do?"

"Dear lady," I answered. "God made Adam, and the Two of Them helped to make Eve—I guess that's why the result's been so uncertain."

"What do you mean?" she asked.

"Adam should never have been let in on

the job," I told her. "A human is sure some machine. I guess he was too much of an amateur, and left out the governor——"

"That's rude!" she cracked out at me.

"The truth's generally a bit that way," I said. "I'm not one to shut my eyes, when it's some one else's sins I'm looking at. I've a strong fellow-feeling for old Sir Almoth. I consider he justified his name. He's some marksman."

"What are you talking? Words or sense?" she asked, honestly bewildered.

"Both," I told her. "If that old amateur, Adam, had only added the governor, Logic, you could have found out all that by yourself. I'll make you a bet, and the amount shall be the sum that you were to have paid me for running your necklace through the Customs —twenty-five thousand dollars."

"What—what do you mean?" she asked, stammering slightly, and turning rather white looking. "What do you want to bet?"

She stared me right in the eyes, closely, and with an intense, expectant attention.

"That you will not manage to run your necklace through by yourself," I said, slowly, looking at her steadily. "I did not ask you to pay me any commission; and I halved what you offered me; but had I arranged to do it for a full five per cent., it would have been money well spent, from your side of the bargain."

She was as white as a sheet now, and had to catch at the forrard bridge-rail, to help steady herself; but I did not spare her; for if I could crush the meanness in her, with the Hammer of Shame, I meant to do so.

"Why had you not the moral strength to tell me the truth, when I worked out for you, how much two and a half per cent. on a million dollars would come to?" I said. "Why did you not just say, simply, that you had not thought to pay so much? I should have relieved you of the bargain in a moment. What is more, I should have respected you for having the moral strength to tell me the truth; though I should have regretted the *trait* of meanness it would have disclosed; for you are a very wealthy woman, and you could well afford to pay me twice what I agreed to run your necklace through for. I did not, as I have said,

ask you to pay me anything. I would have
done it for nothing—just for friendliness'
sake; but when you turned it into a business
proposition, I met you on a business footing.
It was to save your pocket some six hundred
thousand dollars; and for the risk I took of
losing personal liberty, and my situation as
Captain of this ship, I consented to accept
twenty-five thousand dollars as payment.

"And now you have shown not only meanness, but, a thousand times worse, you have
lied to me, lie after lie; and with every lie
you hurt me badly; for you blackened not
only yourself in my eyes; but, at the same
time, you blackened all of your sex; for a
man judges women through the goodness or
badness of the women he gets to know personally. I tell you frankly, Mrs. Ernley, I
wish your necklace had been at the bottom
of the sea, before you had let it be a lever to
further lower my general opinion of all that
you stand for."

"Stop! Stop!" she said, quite hoarsely.
She had flushed once or twice as I set out my
indictment; but now she stood shivering and
deadly pale.

"Help—help me down the steps," she said, and I helped her down to the deck.

"Now leave me," she said, almost in a whisper, "I can manage. No, I will not have you with me. I have done wrong. But I cannot bear you near me. You—you have shamed me so!"

I watched her go along the deck, and pass down one of the stairways, then I went back to the bridge. I do not regret what I have done. I am getting a sick fear that every woman I meet is going to turn out mean or treacherous or deceitful or worse. If I have helped one to cure herself I'm satisfied.

March 19. *Night.*

We docked this morning, and Mrs. Ernley has never come near me once of her own free will. And there has been a deuce of a scene with the Customs.

I did not know, at first, whether to say anything about the necklace, or not; but finally decided that I had better show it, and say it had been left in my charge by a Mrs. Ernley, one of the First Class passengers. If it served to bluff the Customs into sup-

posing that this was the necklace she had
bought, and that she had been swindled into
paying real money for a Carn Prism sham
set of sparklers, it might serve to lull them
from making a drastic search of her. And,
goodness knows, I'm willing enough to do
the little woman a good turn if I can.

When the Chief of the searchers came
along to the chart-house, he asked me a leading question, straight off, which made it sufficiently plain that he knew a good deal
about Mrs. Ernley's Paris transaction.

"Captain," he said, "I hear from one of
our people, who's been aboard, that you and
Mrs. Ernley have got pretty friendly on the
trip across; and I want you to be a real
friend to her; and do your best to persuade
her to show up her necklace, like a wise
woman. We know a good deal about it,
Captain; so, for the Lord's sake, don't try
to do any bluffing, and don't encourage her
to, either. It'll mean serious trouble if you
do. We *know* it's aboard this ship; and we
mean to have it. It's six hundred thousand
dollars of duty we're out for, and we're
going to have it; but she swears she has no

necklace; and my women-searchers haven't been able to locate it yet. Now, will you, Captain, wise her up, that she can't put a thing like this over on us; and I guess we'll let her down easy for false declaration."

"Mister," I said, "perhaps this is what you're looking for;" and I went across and hauled out the sham necklace from a drawer. "She asked me to take care of this for her."

He gave out a little shout of relief; and snatched at the thing. He ran to the North window, and held it up to the light, then he pulled a magnificient looking brilliant from his vest pocket, set in the end of a little steel bar, and he began to compare the "stones" with it.

He let out a sudden exclamation; and whipped an eye-microscope from his pocket. He fitted this to his eye, then turned up the other end of the steel bar, and I saw that there was a "tester" set in it. He scratched carefully with this at one of the "stones" in the necklace. Then he gave a shout of disgust, and turned and hove the necklace on to my chart table.

"Careful with the thing, man!" I said.

"Anyone would suppose you were *blasé!*"

"Careful!" he said. "My oath, Captain, drop it! I don't know whether she's put the blinkers on you too. She may have; though I'm doubting it. But that's not worth more than the platinum setting that mounts the stuff. It's one of those new "prism" fakes. Though, I'll own I never saw such a good one. Now, Captain, we're going to get the real goods; so don't get up against us. Help us, and we'll make things as pleasant as we can; but butt in on us, and you'll get twisted; and the lady'll get prison; for Judge H—— gave it out in court last week that he's going to teach some of these dollar-dames they can't monkey with the U.S.A. laws and get off the way some of them have been doing."

"I'll do my best," I said, "to make things all right. The lady certainly handed me this necklace as the real thing."

I picked it up, and took it across to its drawer; as I did so, there was a knock on the chart-room door, and a Customs officer pushed his head in.

"We've got it, Sir!" he said, in an excited voice. "Miss Synks found it in the ventila-

tor of the lady's cabin. Will you come, Sir?
She's making a rumpus down there. Perhaps the Captain had better come too. Some
of the passengers seem inclined to make
trouble for our people."

The head searcher was already half out
through the doorway, but he beckoned to me
to follow.

When we got down into the main saloon,
off which Mrs. Ernley's cabin opened, I
found there was certainly some riot
going on!

There was a crowd of First Class passengers round her cabin. The door was open,
and over the heads of the passengers, I could
see Mrs. Ernley and a young, smartly-
dressed woman. Mrs. Ernley looked to be
dressed ready for going ashore. She was
standing in the middle of her cabin, and appeared to be holding something frantically
to her breast, which the other woman was
trying to take from her.

At this moment, one of the Customs officials entered the cabin, and went to assist
the woman-searcher in taking from Mrs.
Ernley what she held so crazily to her. Mrs.

Ernley gave out a scream, and at that, there was an ugly growl of sound from the passengers round the doorway.

"Man-handling a lady like that!" I heard one man expostulating, above the sudden murmur of voices.

I reached quickly, and caught the head searcher's elbow.

"For the Lord's sake, sing out to your man to quit mauling the lady," I said, "or there's going to be a lot of unnecessary trouble."

"Svensen," sung out the Chief searcher. "Come out of that!"

At his voice, the semi-circle of passengers glanced round quickly; and I took charge.

"Come, ladies and gentlemen," I said. "This is a matter between Mrs. Ernley and the United States Customs. I am sure you do not want to embarrass her more than need be; so please allow matters to arrange themselves. You can trust me to see that the lady will get courteous treatment, while she's aboard my ship."

"That's the tune, Captain!" called out one of the men passengers. "If this sort of thing is necessary, let it be done properly, I say."

"You may be sure that the head officer and I will show all consideration for the lady," I answered. "He must carry out his duty; but he has no wish to make it more unpleasant than need be. Now do, please, all of you go away from the doorway. There is no need for any scene."

They melted like snow, now that their instinctive desire for fair and courteous treatment for a woman in trouble, had been assured, and I stepped right in through the doorway, and touched the woman-searcher on the shoulder.

"Allow me, one moment," I said. "Perhaps I can get Mrs. Ernley to listen to me, without continuing this painful situation."

The woman-searcher glanced over my shoulder at her Chief, who must have nodded his assent to my intervention; for she loosed hold of Mrs. Ernley, immediately.

"Mrs. Ernley!" I said. "Mrs. Ernley! Please listen to me. You must give the necklace up. You will have to pay the duty; but the Chief searcher has kindly assured me that he will not press any charge against you, if you will consent now to let matters go for-

ward, without further trouble." I looked
over my shoulder at the head officer.

"I am right in making the lady this
promise?" I asked, under my breath. "I
have your promise?"

He nodded. I could see that the man
was genuinely sorry for her; but he had got
to do his duty, which was to see that Uncle
Sam got his full and necessary pound of
meat.

"Now, Mrs. Ernley, please give me the
necklace, and end this distressing scene. It
is distressing us all. We are all genuinely
sorry for you, but you must realize that
luxuries must be paid for; and the Customs
can favour no one. Come now." And, very
gently, I eased her hands open, and took from
her the tightly rolled up glittering string of
stones. She stood then, looking not at me,
but fixedly at the stones, as I held them out
to the head officer. She was trembling from
head to foot, and I beckoned suddenly to
the woman-searcher to hold her; for I
thought she was going to faint.

The head officer let the glimmering string
of light swing a time or two in his hands, as

if he were, himself, fascinated by the flashes they sent out. Then he turned, and put his head out of the cabin doorway.

"Jim," he called, "slip up and fetch Mr. Malch."

"The official appraiser," he explained, turning back to me. "I'll have him on this job; then there sure can't be any error!"

In about two minutes, the man, Jim, returned with Mr. Malch—a long, thin, hard-bitten looking man.

"Hand it across, Soutar," he said, "I'll soon put you wise to the quality of the goods!"

He took it over to the port-hole, and laid it out in the bunk—Mrs. Ernley's own bunk. Then he pulled a case out of his pocket, and bent over the necklace.

I was standing by Mrs. Ernley, talking to her quietly, to try to ease the tension a bit. The woman-searcher, who was evidently the Miss Synks who had found the necklace, had moved behind Mrs. Ernley, ready to support her, if need be. I must say, they were downright considerate to her, taking things all round.

Suddenly, the appraiser burst out into a contemptuous laugh.

"For all sakes, Soutar, aren't you wise to know glass from the real thing!" he said, turning round. He held the necklace out to us all. "There's not a diamond there!" he went on. "It's one of those Carn Prism fakes. If the lady bought this for the real goods, she's been done as brown as a coffee bean!"

Mrs. Ernley let out a shrill scream—

"It's real! It's real! I know it's real! I paid a million dollars for it!" She sprang at the man, and snatched it rudely from his hand.

"Real glass, Madam!" he said, grimly. "I guess you can take that kind of stuff ashore by the cartload, duty free. We ain't going to object! Of course, the setting's fine. It's real platinum; but I guess we're looking for more than settings!"

Mrs. Ernley let the necklace fall with a sharp little clitter of sound, to the floor. And Miss Synks was just in time to catch her, as she fainted.

I helped lift her on to the settee; then I

picked up the condemned necklace, coiled it up and tossed it on to the table.

"Poor little woman!" said the Chief of the searchers. "She's sure been put through a quick-change scene of high-voltage troubles. I guess she's got a sure police-case against that Paris jeweller! That's if they ever put hands on him again, which ain't a likely thing, after cleaning up a million as easy as all that!"

Abruptly, a sudden idea came to him; and I saw suspicion flash into his eyes.

"I'll take another look, Captain Gault, at that necklace you've got in charge for the little lady!" he said, with a little curt note in his voice. "Maybe I made a mistake somewhere. We'll have Mr. Malch on the job. He's the man that knows the real goods."

"Certainly," I said. "Come up to the chart-room."

He beckoned to the appraiser, and we all went to the chart-room. I stepped across to the drawer, and fetched out the first necklace. I handed it to the Appraiser without a word. I was getting a heap weary of it all.

"Same sort of prism muck!" said Mr.

Malch, shrugging his shoulders contemptuously, after a series of tests. "I guess it's the
guy over in Paris that's made the dollars this
trip! Come on, Soutar. Sorry to have both-
ered you, Cap'n; but I guess it's all in the
day's work."

"Just so," I said, as dryly as I could.

After they had gone, I went down to see
how Mrs. Ernley was. She had come round,
when I called, and was helping her maid to
pack. She looked up at me, very white-
faced, and very red eyed.

"Please go way, Captain Gault," she said.
"Thank you for all you've done. I want to
go right away and never see any one again.
I've been a very silly, weak woman. Please
go away."

And of course, I had to go.

But this evening, when all my business
was done, I dressed, and had a taxi sent
down to the ship. I was going up to see
Mrs. Ernley, at her big house up Madison
Square way. I meant to make the returning
of the sham necklace an excuse to call;
though I wondered whether she might not
still refuse to see me.

However, when I sent my name in to her, I found I was to be received, and I went in, wondering how I should find her. She was sitting in a pretty boudoir sort of room; and when I entered, she was playing idly and rather sadly with the other necklace; but as I came into the room she threw it on to a chair, and came across to meet me.

"A million dollars is a lot to lose in one lump," I told her, as she sat down again; "even for a rich woman like you."

"Yes," she said, quietly. "But I guess that's not what I'm feeling worst about, now I've got steadied a bit. I sure showed that I was poor stuff, didn't I, Captain Gault? I guess I've never been so ashamed of myself in my life as I feel right now."

I nodded.

"I'm glad to hear it," I said. "I fancy you've won more than you've lost, if you feel that way, dear lady."

"Perhaps I have," she answered, rather doubtfully, as she reached out for the necklace she had been playing with. "The police here have cabled across; and I guess they'll do their best to nab that crook, Monsieur

Jervoyn, who sold me this rubbish; though I'm not surprised I was taken in. Even the Customs Expert couldn't tell they weren't real, first go off, could he?"

I nodded again.

"Mrs. Ernley," I said, "you've come well out of this affair, in many ways, and I think you've taken it as a bit of a lesson, haven't you?"

"Yes," she said, slowly. "I don't think I shall ever forget what I've gone through to-day; and all the voyage, for that matter. I suppose, Captain Gault, you feel just simple contempt for me. You feel I've proved I was weak. You said I should."

She dabbed at her eyes with her handkerchief. "I suppose being rather well-off *does* make one inclined to grow soft, morally," she murmured at last.

"I guess Life is either Training or Degeneration," I told her. "But smuggling diamonds isn't necessarily degeneration. It consists largely of *using* Circumstances. But it's sure a man's job. A woman's too much given to expecting heads I win, tails you lose. And that's just *dodging* Circumstances. And dodging Circumstances is plain Degeneration."

She nodded.

"I guess you're right, Captain Gault," she said quietly. "A woman's awful apt to think she ought to be able to eat her maccaroons and have them still in her hand. And that's plumb impossible, it seems!"

I stood up, smiling at the pretty, earnest way she mixed her words.

"In this case, dear lady," I said, "the 'plumb impossible' has happened, or something like it. I'll run along now; but you'll like to know that the necklace you've got in your hands is worth just about one million dollars cash; so I'd sure put it away safe to-night before you turn-in."

She had stood up, as I was speaking; and she held the necklace out now in her right hand, and stared first at me, and then back at it, as if she were half dazed with what I had just said to her.

"What?" she asked, at last, in a voice that was low and deep, like a man's with the nerve shock that had half paralyzed her and relaxed her vocal chords. "What?"

"Please sit down," I said, and guided her back gently into her chair. . . . "Now you're all right. . . . Sure?"

She nodded speechlessly at me.

"Listen to me then," I told her. "That's your million-dollar necklace. The actual thing that you bought in Paris. It's genuine and quite all right. I saved it for you. Yes, I'll tell you how.

"When the Customs man came up into my chart-room, I showed him the sham necklace, and he tested it and found it was sham. Then one of his men came up, to say that they had found the real one in your cabin ventilator. I had pretended to put the false one back into one of my chart-room drawers; but really I had coiled it up tight in my hand.

"I followed the Chief searcher down and I coaxed you to hand over the real one, which you had rolled up into a ball in your hands, after you must have snatched it from the woman-searcher.

"Then I handed the Customs man the false necklace, which had been ready in my hand, and kept the real one in its place.

"Of course, they simply found out, for the second time of asking, that the false necklace, was as false as it was! Pretty obvious sort of thing to find. Afterwards, you remember, you snatched it back, when the Expert told you it was only Carn glass, and then you fainted and dropped it on the floor. I helped lift you to the settee; then I picked up the false necklace; wrapped it up, and threw it on to your cabin table; but what I actually threw, was the real one, and kept the false one again in my hand.

"Now, don't you admire my nerve, chucking down on to the table right in front of the Expert, a million-dollar necklace, as if it were just common so-much-a-ton-stuff— eh? Wasn't that a great bluff, dear lady?"

"Sure! Sure! Sure!" she gasped out, her eyes dancing. "And then?"

"And then, I guess I sealed the trick. The Customs man got a sudden notion that he would like to have another look at the necklace I had shown him. in my chart-room.

"Well, I took him up there, along with the Expert, and I went over to the drawer,

dipped in my hand, that held the sham
necklace, and then pulled the thing out, in
a sort of *ad lib.* fashion, for them to examine
for the third time of asking.   They certainly
showed some interest in that length of
prism sparklers! By the way, I've brought
it back for you," and I drew it out of my
pocket and laid it on the table.

Mrs. Ernley rose now and went across to
a small writing desk. I saw a minute later,
that she had started to fill in a cheque; and
I guessed it was my commission.

I walked over to her, and put my hand
across the cheque-book.

"Dear lady," I said, "I can take no commission for what I did. Our business transaction ended when you changed the necklaces. . . . But, out of curiosity, I should
like to know just how much the cheque was
going to be?"

"Look!" she said, and I drew away my
hand, and looked. It was for a hundred
thousand dollars.

"I'm glad!" I told her. "I guess you've
stamped pretty solid on the poor streak in
you. You're sure going to be one of the few

women I can think well of. But I can't take that cheque, dear lady. If you want to go on the way you've begun, send it to the Sailors' Home. They need the cash pretty bad, I know."

Then I shook hands and left; though she begged me to stay; and showed the nicest and best possible side that a woman has to show.

"What a strange man you are, Captain Gault," she said, as I turned and smiled at her in the doorway.

"Maybe!" I said. "All humans are a bit strange to others, when you get the lid off some of their soul pots!"

But when I got out into the street I couldn't help thinking how true my notions of woman often are. Her actions are prompted either by insane meanness, or else by an equally insane generosity!

I guess it's right that old Adam left the governor out!

CHAPTER II

THE DIAMOND SPY

s.s. *Montrose,*
June 18.

I AM having enough bother with one or two of the passengers this trip, to make me wish I was running a cargo boat again.

When I went up on the upper bridge this morning, Mr. Wilmet, my First Officer, had allowed one of the passengers, a Mr. Brown, to come up on to the bridge and loose off some prize pigeons. Not only that; but the Third Officer was taking the time for him, by one of the chronometers.

I'm afraid what I said looked a bit as if I had lost my temper.

"Mr. Wilmet," I said, "will you explain to Mr. Brown that this bridge is quite off his beat; and I should like him to remove himself, and ask him please to remember the fact for future reference. If Mr. Brown wants to indulge his taste in pigeon flying, I've no objections to offer at all; but he'll kindly keep off my bridge!"

I certainly made no effort to spare Mr. Brown; and this is not the first time I have had to pull him up; for he took several of his pigeons down into the dining-saloon yesterday, and was showing them off to a lot of his friends—actually letting them fly all about the place; and you know what dirty brutes the birds are! I gave him a smart word or two before all the saloon-full; and I fancy they agreed with me. The man's mad on his pigeon-flying.

Then there's a bore of a travelling Colonel, who's always trying to invade my bridge, to smoke and yarn with me. I've had to tell him plainly to keep off the bridge, same as Mr. Brown, only, perhaps, not quite in the same manner. And there are two ladies, an old and a young one, who are always on the bridge steps, as you might say. I took the opportunity to talk to the oldest about my eighth boy, to-day. I thought it might cool her off; but it didn't; she's started talking to me now about the dear children; and as I'm not even married, I've lied myself nearly stupid, confound her! And the old lady has let the young one know, *of course!* And the young one has left me now entirely to the old one's mercies! Goodness me!

But the passenger who really bothers me, is a Mr. Aglae, a sallow, fat, darkish man, short, and most infernally inquisitive. He seems always to be hanging about; and I've more than a notion he's cultivating a confidential friendship with my servant-lad.

Of course, I've guessed all along he's a Diamond Spy; and I don't doubt but there's need for the breed in these boats; for there's a pile to be made in running stones and pearls through the Customs.

I nearly broke loose on him to-day and told him, slam out, I knew he was a spy, and that he had better keep his nose out of my cabin and my affairs; and pay a bit more attention to people who had the necessary thousands to deal successfully in his line of goods.

The man was actually peeking into my cabin, when I came up behind him; but he was plausible enough. He said he had knocked, and thought I said, "Come in." He had come to ask me to take care of a very valuable diamond, which he brought out of his vest pocket, in a wash-leather bag. He told me he had begun to feel it might be safer if properly locked up. Of course, I explained that his diamond would be taken care of in the usual way; and when he asked my opinion of it, I became astonishingly affable; for it was plainly his desire to get me to talk on the subject.

"A magnificent stone!" I said. "Why, I should think it must be worth thousands. It must be twenty or thirty carats."

I knew perfectly well that the thing was merely a well cut piece of glass; for I tried it slyly on the tester I carry on the inner edge of my ring; and as for the size, I was purposely "out"; for I knew that if it had been a diamond, it would have been well over sixty carats.

The little fat spy frowned slightly and I wondered whether I'd shown him that he was getting up the wrong tree; and then, in a moment, I saw by the look in his eyes that he suspected me as much as ever; and was putting me down as being simply *ostentatiously* ignorant of diamonds. After he had gone, I thought him over for a bit, and I got wishing I could give the little toad a lesson.

June 19.

I got a splendid idea during the night. We should dock this evening, and I've just time to work it. The diamond-running talk came up at dinner last night, as is but natural in these boats; and different passengers told some good yarns, some of them old and some new, and a lot of them very clever dodges that have been worked on the Customs.

One man at my table told an I.D.B. yarn of how a duck had been induced to gobble up diamonds by bedding them in pellets of bread, and in this way the diamonds had been cunningly hidden, at a very critical moment for the well-being of their "illicit" owner.

This gave me an idea; for that diamond spy has got on to my nerves a bit, and if I don't do something to make him look and feel a fool, I shall just get rude; and rudeness to passengers is not a thing that commends itself to owners.

I have a coop of S. African black ringneck hens, down on the well-deck, which I am taking across to my brother, who makes a hobby of hen-keeping and has bred some wonderful strains.

I sent my servant for a plateful of new crumb-bread, and then I fished out from the bottom of my sea-chest, a box of what we used to call among the islands "native blazers" — that is, cut-glass imitation diamonds, which certainly cleaned up to a very pretty glitter. I'd had the things with me for years, some left-overs, from a sporting trip I made once that way.

I sat down at my table, and made bread pellets; and then I began to bed each of the "stones" into a pellet. As I did so, I became aware that some one was peeping in the window that looks into the saloon. I glanced into the mirror, across on the opposite bulkshead of my cabin, and saw for an instant the face of my servant.

This is what I had expected.

"So ho! my lad!" I said to myself. "I guess this is the last trip you'll take with me; for, though I'll see you aren't dangerous now, you may be some other time."

When I had done coating my "diamonds" with bread, I went forrard to my hen-coop, and began to feed the pellets to the birds. As I turned away from giving the last of the big bread pills, I literally bumped into Mr. Aglae, who had just come round the end of the coop. Obviously, he had received word from my servant, and had been watching me feed diamonds to my hens, so as to hide my illegal jewelry, while the search officers were aboard!

It was rather funny to see the way in which the diamond spy put on a vacant expression, and apologized for his clumsiness, blaming the rolling of the vessel. As a matter of fact, he had no business in that part of the ship at all; and I made a courteous reference to this fact; for I wished him to think that I was disturbed and annoyed by his being there at so (apparently) critical a moment for me.

Later on, when I went into the wireless

room, I found Mr. Aglae sending a wireless; and I sat down on the lounge to write my own message, while Melson (the Operator) was sending.

Instead, however, of writing out my own message, I jotted down the dot and dash iddle-de-umpty of the iggle-de-piggle that the Operator was sending; for it was a private code message, and ran: 17 a y b o z w r e y a a j g o o a v o o 1 o w t p q 2 2 3 2 1 m v n 6 7 a m n t 8 t s .17. aglae. g.v.n.

I smiled; for it was the latest official cypher, and I had the "key" in my pocketbook. It is desirable to have what is popuuarly called "a friend in high quarters." Only my friend is not very high, at least, not highly paid; though his secretarial position gives him access in a certain government office to papers that help him considerably to make both ends meet.

After Mr. Aglae had departed, I took out my "key," and translated the message, while Melson was sending mine. Translated, it was this: "Hens fed on hundreds of diamonds concealed in bread pellets. Better come out in the pilot tug. Shall mark coop.

I must not appear in the case at all. Most important capture of years. 17. Aglae. g. v. n."

This was sent to a private address, merely as a blind; for Mr. Aglae would be of little further use as a diamond spy if he began sending cypher messages to the Head Office! The 17, just before his name, I knew must be his official number; and I was interested, and perhaps a little impressed; for I have heard of the unknown "Number 17" before. He has effected some wonderful captures among the diamond smugglers. I wondered what he might look like, minus what I began now to suspect was both false stomachic appendage, and dyed hair, plus his little, vaguely foreign mannerisms, to suit.

The letters "g.v.n.," which followed the signature, were the inner "keys" to the message; for the cypher is really clever, in that a long message can be sent with a limited number of symbols, by a triplicate reading, according to the use of the various combinations—the working of which the main "key" explains, and which are indicated by the combination letters, which are always written, in this cypher, after the signature.

As I went out of the wireless room, I had a second splendid idea. I got some breadcrumbs as an excuse, and had another walk down to the well-deck to look at my coop of prize chickens, and I came slam on Number 17 (as I now called him to myself) just strolling off.

Now, I had made it plain to him that he had no business down there, and I called to him, to ask him what he was doing again in that part of the ship, after what I had told him in the morning.

I must say that Number 17 has got quite a remarkably sound "nerve" on him.

"I'm sorry, Captain," he said; "but I'd lost my cigarette holder. I knew I'd had it in my fingers when I tumbled against you this morning, and I thought I might have dropped it then."

He held it out to me, between his finger and thumb.

"I found it lying on the deck here," he explained. "A mercy it was not trodden on. I'm thankful much; for I prize it."

"That's all right, Mr. Aglae," I said, and
hid the smile his tricky little foreign flavour
of speech rose in me. As a matter of fact,
if what I've heard is correct, the man is
Scotch, bred and born and reared. It shows
what even a Scotchman can come down to!

After he had gone, with one of his dinky
little bows, I overhauled the hen-coop; but
in a casual sort of way, so that no one, looking on, could suspect I was doing more than
making one of my usual bi-daily visits to my
chuck-chucks, and feeding them with
bread-crumbs.

If I had not read the cypher message, I
should certainly not have discovered the
marks that Mr. Aglae had made on the
coop; they were merely three small dots, in a
triangle, like this . · ., with a tiny 17 in the
centre. The thing had just been jotted
down on one of the legs of the coops with a
piece of sharp-pointed chalk, and it could
have been covered with a ha'penny.

I grinned to myself and went to the car-
penter's shop for a piece of chalk. I made
Chips sharpen it to a fine point with a
chisel; then I put it in my pocket and con-

tinued my afternoon stroll round the decks.

I wanted first to place Mr. Aglae; for it would spoil part of the amusingness of my plot, if he were on the spy, and saw what I was going to do. I found him, away aft in the upper-deck smoke-room, reading *Le Petit Journal,* and looking most subtly foreign and most convincingly innocent.

"You little devil!" I thought; and went right away to the well-deck. Here, in an unobtrusive way, I copied Mr. Aglae's private signature, faithfully, on to the hen-coop above the one in which I was carrying my brother's black ring-necks. The coop was occupied for the voyage by the bulk of Mr. Brown's confounded pigeons, which, I had insisted, must not be brought again into the saloon.

After I had re-duplicated the mark, I lifted out four of my ring-necks from the bottom coop, and put them into the top one, among Mr. Brown's pigeons. My argument was that, when the searchers boarded us with the pilot, they would find both these coops marked, and both with hens in them, and would act accordingly. They would

have to open the upper coop to remove
the four hens, and there would be a general
exodus of Mr. Brown's pigeons, which
would re-double the confusion and general
glad devilment of my little plot.

Mr. Brown would be enormously angry
and enormously vociferous. I could picture
him thundering: "I never heard of such a
thing! Confound you, Sir! I shall write to
The Times about this."

And then, it seemed to me, Number 17
would have to come and make some kind
of semi-public explanation, of what he
could never properly explain; and ever
after, his value as a diamond spy would be
decreased something like twenty-five per
cent.; for quite a lot of people aboard
(maybe some of them in the Diamond-Running business) would be able to get a good
square look at the famous Number 17, and
for all time afterwards, in whatever way he
might try to veil his charming personality,
he would run chances of being recognised
at some awkward and premature moment;
at least, from his point of view!

But, of course, at first, Mr. Aglae (Number 17) would be only partly involved in my cheerful little net of difficulties. He would know, all the time, that these curious complications were only trifling; for had he not made the greatest capture of years. Let Mr. Brown be apologized to; even compensated, if such compensation were legally his right. The great thing would be to reduce the black ring-necks to poultry, as speedily as possible, and then to pick his Triumph from their gizzards!

I wriggled quietly with pleasure, as I saw it all. And then, the Official Appraiser's brief explanation to the Chief; and the salty flavour of the Chief's explanation to Number 17, that there was no law against a sea Captain feeding his pet hens with bits of glass, cut or otherwise, for the improvement, or otherwise, of their digestions.

Then there would be the replacing of my five dozen ring-necks, or their equivalent in good honest dollars, treasury dollars, I presume. I calculated rapidly that even as the prestige of Number 17 must come down, so the price of my hens should as infallibly go up.

I snicked the lesser door of the upper
coop shut, and watched my four hens and
Mr. Brown's pigeons. The hens clucked,
and walked odd paces in the dignified and
uncertain fashion affected by all hens of a
laying age. The pigeons fluttered a bit, and
then resumed their wonted cooing; and
after that, all was comfortable in that ark;
for the hens discovered pigeon-food to be
very good hen-food also, and set to work
earnestly to fill the unfillable.

*   *   *   *

The searchers came aboard with the Pilot,
and after the usual preliminaries, my pres-
ence was requested at the opening of the
hen-coop. I noticed that Mr. Aglae was
still in the upper smoke-room, as I passed,
and there he appeared intent to stay. I admired his judgment.

The officials gathered on the well-deck,
and the Chief explained that they had received certain information which they were
acting upon; and asked me formally
whether I had any diamonds to declare.

"I'm sorry to say that I've left my diamond investments at home this trip, Mister,"

I said. "I've nothing I'm setting out to declare, except you've been put on to some mare's nest!"

"We happen to think otherwise, Cap'n," he said. "I've given you your chance, and you've chucked it. Now you've got to take what's coming to you!"

He turned to one of his men.

"Open the lower coop, Ellis," he told him. "Rake out those chickens. Hand 'em over to the poulterer."

As each chicken was taken out, it was handed to the poulterer, and the man killed it then and there. My little plan was making things unfortunate, of course, for my brother's ring-necks; but, after all, they were fulfilling their name, and I felt that, eventually, I should have nothing personally to grumble about.

But, in spite of this pleasant inward feeling, I protested formally and vigorously against the whole business, and pointed out that someone would have to pay, and keep on paying for an "outrage" (as I called it) of this kind.

The Chief merely shrugged his shoulders,

and told the men to rake out the four hens from the upper coop. The man reached in his hand through the trap; but, of course, the hens side-stepped him in a dignified fashion. Then the man grew a little wrathy, and whipped down the whole front of the coop, and plunged in, head and shoulders, to get them.

Instantly, what I had planned, happened. There was a multitudinous, harsh, dry whisper of a hundred pairs of wings; and then, hey! the air was white with pigeons. The man backed out of the coop, with a couple of my ring-neck hens in each hairy fist; and met the blast of his superior's wrath—

"You clumsy goat!" snarled the Chief— "What——" And then the second thing that I had foreseen, occurred.

"Confound you, Sir!" yelled Mr. Brown, dashing in among us, breathless. "Confound you! Confound you! You've loosed all my pigeons! What the blazes does this mean! What the blazes. . . ."

"You may well ask, Sir, what it means," I answered. "I think these officials have gone mad!"

But Mr. Brown was already, to all appearances, quite oblivious of anyone or anything, except his beloved pigeons.

He had lugged out a big gold watch and a notebook and was making frantic efforts to achieve a lightning-like series of time-notes, staring up with a crick in his neck, trying crazily to identify the directions taken by various of his more particular birds.

He had, of course, to give it up almost at once; for already the bulk of the birds had made their preliminary circles, and were now shooting away for the coast, at various angles.

Then Mr. Brown proved himself more of a man than I had hitherto supposed possible in one who flew pigeons. He attained a height of denunciatory eloquence, which not only brought most of the first-class passengers to the spot; but caused a number, even of the married women, to withdraw hastily.

The Chief made several attempts to pacify him; but it was useless, and he made dumb-show then to the poulterer to set about opening up my brother's five dozen ring-necks, which that man did with admirable skill, until the well-deck looked like a slaughter house. And still Mr. Brown continued to express himself.

At last, the Chief sent a messenger, and (evidently much against his will) Mr. Aglae had to come and explain.

Mr. Brown ceased to denunciate for a moment, while Mr. Aglae explained, and the passengers crowded nearer, until the Chief asked me to tell them to retire. But I shrugged my shoulders. It fell in well with my plans for the spy's flattening, to have as many witnesses as possible.

"I never marked your coop, Sir," said Number 17, warmly. "It was the Captain's coop of hens that I marked. . . ."

"Rubbish!" interpolated the Chief; "here's your mark on both coops!"

It struck me, in that moment, that possibly the Chief would not be sorry to weaken Number 17's position; for that man may have been climbing the promotion-ladder a little too rapidly for the Chief's peace of mind; though I knew the Chief would not dare say much, in case the capture proved as important as Number 17 had described.

I never saw a man look so bewildered as the spy, when he saw that both coops were marked. Then he turned and looked straight at me; but I gave him a good healthy back-stare.

"So," I said aloud, for every one to hear, "you're a beastly spy? I don't wonder I've felt crawly every time you've passed near me this trip!"

The little man glared at me, and I thought he was going to lose control, and come for me; but at that moment, Mr. Brown, having rested, began again.

During the fluent period that followed, the poulterer worked stolidly and quickly and I saw that he was resurrecting quite a number of my cut-glass ornaments.

They had brought out the official appraiser with them; so important had they considered the case, from Number 17's message; and that man, breaking himself from the charmed circle of Mr. Brown's listeners, walked over to the poulterer, and began to examine the "diamonds."

I watched him, quietly, and saw him test the first one, carefully; then frown, and pick up another.   At the end of five minutes, both he and the poulterer finished their work almost simultaneously; and I saw the appraiser throw down the last of the "diamonds" contemptuously on to the hatch.

"Mr. Franks!" he called out aloud, to the Chief, "I have to report that there is not a single diamond in the crops of these—er— poultry.   There are a large number of pieces of cut-glass, such as can be bought for ten cents a dozen; but no diamonds.   I imagine our Mr. Aglae has made a thumper for once."

I grinned, as I realized that Number 17 was not loved, even by the appraiser.   But I laughed outright, when I looked from the Chief's face to Number 17's, and then back again.

Mr. Brown had halted spasmodically, in his fiftieth explanation of the remarkable and unprintable letter that he meant to write to *The Times,* on the subject of his outrage. And now he commenced again, but, by mutual consent, everyone moved away sufficiently far to hear themselves speak; and there and then, the Chief said quite some of the things he was thinking and feeling about Number 17's "capture."

Number 17 said not a word. He looked stunned. Abruptly, a light came into his eyes, and he threw up his hand, to silence the Chief.

"Good Lord, Sir!" he said, in a high, cracking voice of complete comprehension. "The pigeons! The pigeons! We've been done brown. The hens were a blind worked off on me, to keep me from smelling the pigeon pie. Carrier pigeons, Sir! *What* a fool I've been!"

I explained that he had no right to make such a libellous and unfounded statement, and Mr. Brown's proposed letter to *The Times* grew in length and vehemence. Eventually, Mr. Aglae had to apologise as publicly as he had slandered both Mr. Brown and me. But that did not prevent us from presenting our bills for compensation for damage done. And what is more, both of us got paid our own figure; for neither the Treasury, nor its officers, were eager for the further publicity which would have inevitably accompanied the fighting of our "bills of costs" at a court trial.

   *   *   *   *

It was, maybe, a week later, that Mr. Brown and I had dinner together at a certain very famous restaurant.

"Pigeons——" said Mr. Brown, meditatively—"I like 'em best with a neat little packet of diamonds fixed under their feathers."

"Same here!" I said, smiling reminiscently.

I filled my glass.

"Pigeons!" I said.

"Pigeons!" said Mr. Brown, raising his glass.

And we drank.

CHAPTER III

s.s. *Iolanthe,*
October 29.

I MET a rum sort of customer ashore in 'Frisco to-day. At least, I was the customer, and he, as a matter of fact, was the shopman. It was one of those Chinese curio shops, that have drifted down, somehow, near to the water front. By the look of him, he was half Chinaman, a quarter negro, and the other quarter badly mixed. But his English was quite good, considering.

"You go to England, Cap'n?" he asked me.

"London Town, my lad," I told him. "But you can't come. We don't carry passengers. Try higher up. There's a passenger packet ahead of my ship; you'll see her with the prettily painted funnel."

"I not want to come," he explained. Then he came a step nearer to me, and spoke quieter, taking a look quickly to right and left; but there was no one else in the shop.

"Want to send a blox home, Cap'n—a big long blox. Long as you, Cap'n," he told me, almost in a whisper. "How much you take him for? Send him down to-night, when dark?"

"Who've you been murdering now?" I said, lighting a cigarette. "I should try the bay, and have a good heavy stone or two in the sack. I'm not in the body-hiding line."

The man's yellow dusky face went quite grey, and his eyes set, for an instant, in a look of complete terror. Then some sense of comprehension came into them, and he smiled, in rather a pallid kind of way.

"Yo mak-a joke, Cap'n," he said. "I not murder any one. The blox contain a mummy, I have to consign to the town of London."

But I had seen the look on his face, when I let off my careless squib about the corpse; and I know when a man's badly frightened.

Also, why did he not consign his box of mummy to London in the ordinary way; and why so anxious to send it aboard after dark? In short, there were quite a number of whys. Too many!

The man went to the door, and took a look out, up and down the street; then came away, and went to the inner door, which I presumed was his living-room. He drew back and shut the door gently; then took a walk round the backs of the counters, glancing under them. He came out, and walked once or twice up and down the centre of the shop, in a quick, irresolute kind of way, glancing at me earnestly. I could see that his forehead was covered with sweat, and his hands shook a little, as he fumbled his long coat-fixing. I felt sorry for him.

"Now, my son," I said at last, "what is it? You look as if you badly needed to tell somebody. If you want to hand it on to me, I'll not swear to help you; but I'll hold my tongue solidly afterwards."

"Cap'n, Sir," he said, and seemed unable to get any further. He went again to the shop door and looked out; then once more to the inner door, which he opened quietly. He peeped in; then closed it gently, and turned and walked straight across to me. I could see his mind was pretty well made up. He came close up to me, and touched a charm which I wear on my chain.

"That, Cap'n!" he said. "I too!" And he pulled aside a flap of his coat-robe, and showed me a similar one.

"They can be bought for a couple of dollars, anywhere," I said, looking him slam in the eyes. As I said so, he answered a sign I had made.

"Brother," he said. "Greatly good is God to have send you in my distress;" and he answered my second sign.

"Brother," I said, as I might have spoken to my own brother, "let us prove this thing completely." And, in a minute, I could no longer doubt at all. This stranger, part Chinese, part negro and part other things, was a member of the same brotherhood to which I belong. Those who are also my brothers will be able to name it.

"Now," I said, "tell me all your tale, and if it is not against common decency to help you, you may depend on me." I smiled at him encouragingly.

The man simply broke down, and cried a few moments into his loose sleeve.

"You take the blox, Cap'n Brother," he said, at last. "I pay you a t'ousand dollars now this moment."

"No," I told him. "Tell me all about it, first. If it is murder, I can't help you, unless there are things to excuse you; for if you have murdered, you have no longer any call on me, as a brother."

"I not done murder, Cap'n Brother," he said. "I tell you all. You then take blox for t'ousand dollars?"

"If you're clear of anything ugly in this matter," I said, "I'll take your box into hell and out again, if necessary, and there'll be no talk of pay between us. Now get going."

He beckoned to me, and took me round the counter. Here was a long box, a huge affair, very strongly made, and with a hinged lid. He took hold of the lid, and lifted it.

"The mummy!" I exclaimed; for the thing was plain there before my eyes, in its

long, painted casing—a huge man or woman
it must have been, too.

"My son, Cap'n Brother," said the Chinaman.

"What?"

"Him there," said the Chinaman.

"What! Now?" I asked again, staring.

He nodded, and glanced round the shop,
anxiously.

"Dead!" I said. "Is he embalmed?"

"No, Cap'n Brother," he said. "The
mummy-case empty. My son under there,
hiding. Him sleep with much opium I give
him. I ship him to you to-night. First I
tell you why—

"I belong to the Nameless Ones, we call
them. They are a brotherhood also, an'
have live for two t'ousand years. I belong
also with two other brotherhood; for in
China I have importance by family and
relation. But this have to do with the
brotherhood of the Nameless Ones. My son
a little wild. Him drink Engleesh spirit,
an' him come home drunk an' there three of
the Nameless Ones brotherhood speak secret
with me; but him drunk an' not heed noth-

ing. Him come in an' sit down an' laugh.
The Number 7, that is the President, order
him to go out, an' him put the thumb to his
nose—so! The President have a great
anger; but hold it; for I am old in the brotherhood, an' the young man is my son; but
not of the brotherhood.

"The President again order my son to
go; an' my son, in the badness of his great
drunk, him" (the man bent and literally
whispered the terrible detail to me), "him
pull the hair tail of the President, an' the
tail a false one, which I not know before, an'
the tail come away in the hand of my son,
an' the President naked there before us.

"The President wish to kill my son immediately; but I had great speech with him,
an' reasoned much, an' he consent the young
man grow first sober, an' afterward be tried
by the Second Sixty of the brotherhood of
the Nameless Ones that have live two t'ousand year.

"This was yesterday, an' when they gone
away, I put my son to grow sober, an' I prepare the mummy-case to hold him, an' when
him sober, I tell him, an' him nearly die

with great fear; for they will take out his heart, an' hang it in a gold ball over the door of our great Hall; for memory of so great a rude to the President of the brotherhood that is older in all China than all.

"Then I tell my son, I have escape planned for him. I give him strong opium drink an' put him in the mummy-case.

"This happen day before yesterday. In the night, they come for my son; but I tell them him not here. Him away to drink again. They say I hide him. If they find I hide him, they dis-bowel me for a false brother. I say I not hide him. I tell them search house. They search house; but not think of mummy-case; for mummy long in my shop, an' real; but I burn mummy when I prepare case for my son; an' mummy cost five t'ousand dollars. But I care not, for it save my son.

"They have brothers that make a search all drink saloon in 'Frisco. They have a hundred, two hundred to look for my son that make rude to the President of the Nameless Ones that have live for two t'ousand year. But they find him not.

"Then they put a brother here in my house to keep watch, an' a brother in the street, an' how shall I save the life of my son?

"Then you come in Cap'n Brother, an' I see the sign upon your coat, an' you Eng-leesh, an' I have a new courage an' I tell you. An' all you now know."

"Good Lord!" I said. "I've heard of the Nameless Ones, but you don't tell me they'll kill a lad, just for pulling the pigtail of their beastly old President?"

"Hush! Cap'n Brother!" said the man, white with fear, and staring first at the door behind him and then at the outer doorway. "You not speak so, Cap'n. You go now. I not want them to see me talk to you. I send blox down to-night, when dark."

"I'll go when I've satisfied myself on one or two points, brother," I said. I walked straight across the room, and gently opened the inner door and peeped. I wished to test this extraordinary tale. It sounded so un-reasonable to my West-built brain and con-stitution; though I knew there was a good chance of it being every word true.

Well, what I saw in there, quite satisfied me. There was the biggest Chinaman I ever saw in my life, sitting cross-legged on a cushion on the floor, and across his knees he held the longest and ugliest-looking knife I've set eyes on, before or since.

I shut the door, even quieter than I opened it; and when I turned to my new friend, his face was like a gray mask, and he couldn't speak for nearly a minute.

"It's all right, brother," I said; "he never saw me. I'd got to double-prove that tale of yours, before I got mixed up with it. I believe it now, right enough; only it's hard to understand there's a live devil, and this kind of devilry going on, not twenty fathoms away from my own ship."

"You—you take him, Cap'n Brother, you promise true?" he managed to get out, at last; his one thought for that son of his.

"Yes," I said; "but you've not got to bring him aboard to-night. Why, if what you say is right, they'd guess in half a tick; and then it would be too late, except to bury him. You leave it to me, I'll think out a way. I'll send my Second Mate up later to buy one of those bamboo curio sticks of yours. He'll give you a note, telling you what I want you to do. You can read English?"

He nodded, and pointed to the open doorway, at the same time, staring in a stiff sort of terror over his shoulder at the closed door.

The handle of the closed door was being revolved slowly and noiselessly; and I thought it best to get outside at once; for if that big devil inside had grown suspicious, it would increase my difficulties, if he got a sufficient sight of my face to be able to recognize me again.

Later, same day.

My ship is almost across the road, as you might say, from the Chinaman's shop. I'm not eighty yards away, in a direct line; but there's the puffing billy tracks in between—an amusing little way they have here of running their railway lines along the open street!

When I came aboard, I went into my chart house, on the bridge, and reached down a pair of decent glasses, that I got

from the Board of Trade for a little life-
saving stunt I was once mixed up in. I'll
say this for them, they're good glasses, and
I suppose I couldn't match them under sixteen guineas. Anyway, they showed me
what I wanted; for I unscrewed a couple of
the port lights on the shore side of the chart
house, and a couple forrard and aft; and I
kept a watch on that curiosity shop the
whole blessed afternoon, into the evening,
from two to eight.

Standing inside there, I was able to stare
all I wanted, without being seen; and here
is what my afternoon's work told me.

First of all, Mr. Hual Miggett was the
name above the door of my new-found
brother of mixed nationalities. Second, Mr.
Hual Miggett had evidently no idea of the
elaborateness of the watch that was being
kept upon his premises. Apparently there
was no doubt at all, but that the famous
brotherhood of the Nameless Ones depre-
cated strongly the tonsorial attentions of
Master Hual Miggett; for they were out in
force. Through my glasses, I counted more
than a dozen Chinamen in the street, some

lounging about, others walking at the normal Chinese patter pace, and crossing and recrossing one another.

There were two private cars also in the street, drawn up, each with a Chinese driver. (There are some rich men in this affair, I can see that.)

I was easily able to test that these men were there on watch; for they never left the street; also, from time to time, I caught odd vague signs, passing between this one and that. There was obviously *purpose* behind it all.

At five o'clock, I rang down to the steward to send me up my tea; and I ate it there in the chart-house, while I watched.

It came on dusk before seven-thirty; and I noticed that there were more Chinamen in the street, and also there were now three open cars, all driven by Chinamen. I still could not see the need for all this fuss over the President's false pigtail; but, as I explained to myself, there's no accounting for a Chinaman's way of looking at things.

The electrics had been turned on at 7 p.m., and the street was pretty light; though there

were plenty of shadows in places, and
wherever there was a shadow there seemed
to be a Chinaman.

A devil of a lot of chance there would
have been to cart that box out of the shop
and aboard, I thought to myself! The man
must have been made foolish with terror to
think it could be done *that* way. Why, it is
evident these men will keep watch all night,
for a week of Sundays, until they get what
they're after.

At a quarter to eight, I sent the Second
Mate ashore, with a note to Hual Miggett.
I told the Chinaman that if he watched the
street for a bit, he'd find there was a round
score of the "Nameless" devils eyeing his
house; and that if he wanted to bury his
son without delay, he had only to send him
across in the mummy-case, whenever he
liked! I suggested, though, that if he
wished to save the life of his amateur barber,
he had better keep his son comfortably in
the shop, drugged according to need, and
wait for me in the morning, when I would
come along in, and propose a plan by which
he might be gotten safely aboard.

I explained sufficient to my Second Mate to insure his not making a mess of things. I told him that he had better take a cut up into the city first, and come down on the shop from another direction. Then hand over the note, buy a curio stick, and come out at once. After which he had better put in an hour or two at one of the music halls, before returning to the ship, for I do not want that crowd of Chinks in the street to connect me with the shop over the way, as the pork butcher said.

October 30.

I watched the street last night again, from nine up to one o'clock this morning; and there were Chinamen there, either walking past each other or standing about. And every once in a while a car would drive up and stop for an hour at a time, by the corner of the next block, where they could see Hual Miggett's shop.

The Second Mate got aboard, just before I turned in. I had seen him enter and leave the shop, a little after nine, and through my glasses I had traced a couple of Chinamen

follow him right up the street, after he came
out of the shop; but they had turned back,
at last, evidently satisfied that he was simply
a normal customer.

I asked the Second Mate whether anyone
had been in the shop when he delivered the
note.   He said no; but that the biggest
Chinaman in the world had suddenly shoved
his head in through a doorway at the back
of the shop, while he was buying the stick,
and stared steadily at him for nearly a
minute.

"I could have thought he wasn't right in
his head!" the Second Mate told me.   "If
he'd been a bit smaller I should have asked
him what the devil he wanted.   But he was
such an almighty great brute that I took no
notice.   Do you reckon he'd be the man you
saw in the back parlour with the big knife
on his lap?"

"I shouldn't be surprised," I said.

"Just what I thought," remarked the
Second.   "If I were you, Sir, I'd drop the
whole business.   They're a murdering lot of
devils, are Chinamen!   Think nothing at all
of cutting a throat!"

"I agree with your reading of 'em," I said. "But I'll see this difficulty through."

Later on to-day, I went up into the city, where I arranged one or two things; then I went into Jell's, the costumiers, and got them to fix me up with dye and a little careful face paint. Also, they lent me a suit of clothes to match. I'm getting pretty earnest now in this particular bit of business.

When I went in, I was my ordinary self —hair and beard a little brightish; not red. I'm not really what an unprejudiced man would call red. My eyebrows are a couple of shades lighter; and skin fair, reddish. I was dressed in serge, with uniform buttons, and a peak hat. When I came out, my beard, moustache, and eyebrows were dyed black (washable dye, of course). My skin was a good tawny brown, and I had on a check suit that was a chess-knut in every sense of the word; also a crush hat, and spats on my boots. I was the American conception of a certain type of English tourist. God help the type. They would need it.

I called in at a book-shop, and bought a 'Frisco guide, one of those pretty little flip-

flap things that ripple out a fathom long,
all pictures of Telegraph Hill and the water
front and the ferry boats, with glimpses of
the bay and a "peep at Oakland"; not forgetting even the mud flats across the bay,
where the wind-jammers used to lie up by
the dozen and wait for a rise in the grain
freights.

Then I made a line for the water front,
with my "guide" draped over my hands,
staring at it like a five year old laddie.

Presently, as I went along, I stopped outside the Chinaman's shop.   I stared in at
the lacquer boxes; the bamboo walking
sticks, the josses, ... Birmingham de-
lightful variations of certain heathen deities.
I was profoundly impressed.   At least, I
hope I looked like it.   Secretly, I was even
more amused; for I know just sufficient
about what I might call "godology" to recognize the fantastic impossibilities that Ig-
norance had produced, and inflicted daily
upon the unwary.   There were gods there,
whose every "line" should have told a tale,
or made a hidden (often obscene) suggestion to the less Ignorant; but the "lines" or

gagules were meaningless and confused; exactly as an ignorant negro's attempts to reproduce the handwriting of a letter written in English would probably seem to our comprehending eyes. Yet not all was Brummagem.

I have mentioned my staring at the gods; because it was while doing so that I got the first clear idea of how to deal with a certain phase of the situation in which Hual Miggett found himself.

I walked into the shop, and Hual Miggett came forward to serve me. He looked a bilious, dusky yellow, and as if he were at the end of his tether of endurance.

"I would like to look at some of those gods in your window," I said, in a rather high-pitched voice. "I'm always interested in things of that kind."

The mixed-breed crossed to the window, without a word, and drew back the glass partition. I could see that, temporarily at any rate, he had lost all the money-craving of the salesman, and was, for the time being, little more than a living automaton.

As he pulled back the partition, he made

a gesture with his hand, inviting me to look
at the gods, and take my choice. He appeared still too stupefied and weary and
stonily depressed to use any sort of art to
make a sale.

I followed his invitation, and picked up
first one god and then another, looking curiously at their Birmingham craftsmanship.
Finally, I lifted a bronze Goat god that had
first attracted me. It is rare, and should be
worth something.   I glanced up at Hual
Miggett; but he was not even looking at me.
He seemed to be listening, with a frightened, half-desperate look on his flattish face.
Then, with a muttered excuse, he stepped
across the shop and went behind the counter. I guessed he had heard, or fancied he
had heard, a sound from his son in the
mummy-case.

While he was away, I studied the gagules, or "lines," on the Goat god.   They
told me many decidedly unprintable things,
which were extremely interesting, though
repellent to the more restrained individu-
ality of the modern and balanced person.

I examined the "lines" round the base of

the figure, and found the old secret sign "to open," with a chased diminishing device of double lessening circles, leading the eye towards the locations of the concealed catches. I concluded that the boss of the human ankle bone, above the Goat's foot, and the significant inturned thumb of the third hand, might be worth investigating. I pressed on the boss of the protruding ankle-bone, and pulled the thumb, first to me, then pressed it away. As I did so, the bottom of the figure fell away into my hand, and showed an opening into the god, easily big enough to contain my head; for the god is nearly three feet high, and quite two in breadth.

There was nothing in the cavity, and I pressed back the "lid" into place, where it snapped home with a faint double click. As I did so, Hual Miggett came round the counter again into sight, looking a little less anxious. As he walked towards me, I made a certain sign to him, and he stopped and shivered a little, in bewilderment and doubt. Then he answered the sign.

"Brother," I said, speaking quietly in my

natural voice; and I gave him a further sign. And so, in a moment, he knew me.

I said nothing to him about the secret opening into the Goat god. If Hual Miggett did not know his business well enough to read the gagules, it was to no interest of mine to teach him. I continued to turn the god about, as if examining it; but all the time I did so, I was speaking, telling him my plan.

"To-night," I said, "you must give no more than a little opium to your son. In the morning, I will enter with a lady on my arm. The lady and I will examine your curios. Presently, she will throw off her dress, and hat and veil. Underneath, she, or rather he, for it will be a man, will appear dressed in a suit of your son's, which you must get for me now. When all is ready, we will make sufficient noise in the shop to bring out the big Chinaman with the knife, who keeps watch in your inner room. Before, however, he can reach this man, who will seem to him your son, the man (who is an athlete) will race out of your shop; run straight across to the water-side, and jump into a racing launch which will be there, with her engine running. The big man will be sure to follow him, and every one of the watchers in the street will do the same.   The man, however, will be already on his way to Oakland, across the water, and, barring accidents, should be over long before any of them are able to get another launch.

"Meanwhile, we shall have pulled your son out of the mummy-case, and while he is behind the counter, we will get him into the woman's dress, and put the hat and veil on him. I will then take him out of the shop, on my arm, and across to my vessel, while every one's attention is taken up by the escape of the trained runner they imagine to be your son.

"Your son will be weak, with the drugging he has undergone; but he will have my arm; and the distance to my ship is not great. Am I clear?"

"Clear as the moon, Cap'n Brother, when there are no clouds," said the Chinaman. "Truly——"

"One moment," I said. "Perhaps your ecstasy may be calmed a little by learning

that this business will cost you not one cent
less than a thousand dollars, plus the price
of your son's passage to England. The
man who takes the risk will not do it for
less. I have already paid him five hundred
on account, and the second five hundred I
am to pay him to-morrow, if all goes well."

Hual Miggett made no bones about the
money. He pulled a wad of bills out of his
coat-robe; and counted me out one thousand
dollars.

"His passage money will run a hundred
and fifty," I said. "That's what the Company charged last trip to a German hoodoo,
who took the voyage home with us."

He paid me this also, while I continued
to revolve the Goat god in my hands, as if
I were really in doubts whether to buy it,
or not. This was in case we were watched.
Finally, I asked him seriously what he
wanted for it, as I have a weakness for that
kind of thing.

As I spoke, I saw the money greed show
momentarily in his eyes.

"One t'ousand dollars," he said.

It was worth, perhaps, five or six hundred, and as much more as he could get for it, as per Curio Dealers' Creed; but I did not bother to argue with him. His sudden touch of meanness, considering the trouble and risk I was taking for his sake, sickened me a bit; and I simply put the god back on the shelf, without a word.

"The suit of clothes," I said; and Hual Miggett went out of the shop. As he did so, I slipped across and looked into the box at the mummy-case. It belonged evidently to the 18th Dynasty. It was black, with crossed hands carved in relief upon the breast, and the mask was a dull red.

I lifted the upper half quickly, and looked inside; and in that moment, I believed that Hual Miggett's son was not hidden in the mummy-case at all; for instead of the living body of a young Chinaman, I found, apparently, the thoroughly dead body of a mummy, all wound round and round eternally with age-browned bandages. The head and face of the mummy were wrapped tightly with the same brown bandages, in a way that precluded any idea of a living, breathing being within.

And then, as I stared, I realized that the thing was alive. The breast was stirred ever so faintly under its swathings. It gave me a simply beastly feeling, for a moment, to watch it. Then, suddenly, I saw how the whole thing had been worked and I stooped and caught at one of the tightly stretched, age-stiffened folds of the encircling bandages. I lifted, and the whole of the bandages came away, in a life-size half model of the human body.

Cunning Hual Miggett! I saw how he had managed this most clever method of suggesting that the figure below the bandages was really *wrapped* in them. You see, if you take a mummy, and, with a sharp knife, very carefully cut through the bandages, down each side, working right round the mummy, from head to feet, it is possible, sometimes, to work the brown, ancient bandages free from the mummy, so that they come away in two half shells (back and front) which, having become stiffened by age and olden spices, are a veritable and exact model of the mummy they have so long enwrapped.

Clever Hual Miggett! He had cut the bandages free from what I might term their original owner, in two full length halves, then, having, as he had informed me, destroyed the mummy, he had laid his son in the lower half of the hardened shape of wrappings, and placed the other half upon the top of him, so that it appeared to any one looking into the mummy-case that it enclosed only an incredibly olden figure, wrapped in bandages untouched for many and many a forgotten century.

Breathing had been arranged for by a few hidden slits, and the mummy-case and outer box had been similarly doctored.

No wonder the searching Chinese had never "tumbled" to his hiding-place, when they searched the shop!

I lifted the body-shaped skin of brown bandages right out of the case and looked in. There was a sallow young Chinese-looking man inside, lying in a heavily drugged and extremely unwashed condition. The shaped shell of bandages was long, much longer than the young Chinaman, and in the space at his feet, under a piece of fancy sacking, there was the most magnificent carving I could ever have dreamed of, in old amber, of the nameless god, Kuch, of the Blood Lust.

There is no actual name for this Monstrosity; which is, indeed, indicated only by a curious ugly guttural. It is known literally as the Nameless One. There is no real equivalent in the letter sounds of any nation for the guttural which indicates this embodiment of the most dreadful of the Desires — the elemental appeal of the Blood Lust—a lust that has been atrophying through weary centuries, under the effects of the Codes of Restraint, which are more popularly termed Religion.

As I have said, there is no symbol, or written equivalent, in any language for the indicating guttural of this truly terrible deifying of the most monstrous of the primitive Desires; so that the crudely phonetic "Kuch" has become, literally, the name by which Western writers have alluded to it, in dealing with the frightful lore which concerns this embodiment of all that is behind every brutish Impulse of man.

And here, before my eyes, was a marvel-lously wonderful representation of the Blood Monster, carved from one enormous lump of yellow amber; with every last detail of typified vileness, reproduced with an amazingly wonderful and horrible skill of workmanship.

*   *   *   *

I replaced the various covers quickly, and hurried outside the counter again; for I had heard a sound that might have been the big brute of a Chinaman moving in the inner room.

I resumed my broken inspection of the big, bronze Goat god; and presently, as I turned it this way and that, I was aware that the handle of the door of the inner room was turning quietly. Then the door slowly opened, and the enormous head of the big Chinaman came forward into the shop, star-ing round. He stared like a great animal; and moved his monstrous, ugly head and flat, brutish face from side to side, just as I have seen a dangerous bull swing his head, before charging.

I had a feeling that the man reminded me

of something; and suddenly I realized that his face, in some uncomfortable, unnatural way, suggested that of the god I had discovered at the feet of the man in the mummy-case. And it was just then, in that instant, that I comprehended the full extent, shape and quality of the dangerous business into which I was poking my Western nose.

"Oh, you rotten liar, Hual Miggett!" I said to myself. "You rotten liar, to have let me in for all this!"

It had come like a flash; but I had been pretty sure, since discovering the abnormal excitement among the Chinamen (made evident in the number and type of those who watched the house), that there was something more troubling them than what I might term pulled pigtail.

It was this suspicion which had made me step across to the mummy-case as soon as Hual Miggett had gone for a suit of his son's Chinese garments. The god, the Nameless One, was the real hub about which the chief excitement was twiddling. I wondered I had not seen it on the instant; but it was plain enough now—the brotherhood of the Nameless Ones; and the Nameless god! It was, at once, so obvious what the brotherhood was named after! And the Representation of the "Kuch" in yellow amber was undoubtedly the amazingly valued possession of the brotherhood.

The pulling of the President's pigtail was all a clever but outrageous lie (oh, you liar, Hual Miggett!). The young Miggett had evidently displayed no such tonsorial leanings as his father had suggested. Burglary (preferably of valuable "godlike" curios) was evidently his *forte!* Being so confoundedly mixed of birth, I presume he had no especial fears of a god so essentially Chinese in conception!

And I had been hauled into the business as a sort of *édition de luxe* of the Cat's Paw. . . . Not much! I can understand Hual Miggett, senior, being so eager to send mummy-case, and all, abroad. But if I save his son to-morrow, the god shall certainly not come with us. I guess he deserves the worry of it!

At this point, much to my relief, the considerably overgrown member of the brotherhood withdrew himself as noiselessly as he had intruded. I wondered what dreadful things the brute could tell of untellable Rites; and while I was wondering this, Hual Miggett returned.

I took the two garments and the funny little cap from him, and nodded towards the inner door.

"Monsieur the High Chief Executioner of the brotherhood has just stuck his ugly head into the shop," I told him.

The man went ghastly in color, and stared at me, as if I were something superhuman. I began to think my shot must have got a bulls-eye.

"I don't know what you're doing, mixed up with people of that kind," I told him. Then I stuffed the garments (they were very thin material) into my inside pockets, and the cap I folded small, and slipped under my belt; for I was not going out of that shop, carrying any parcel of a size sufficiently large to make the watchers suspect me of being used as a vehicle for the conveying of their beastly god to some other place. I guessed I should have a bad accident, before

I had gone the length of the street, if any of them got thinking that!

"To-morrow, about ten in the morning," I said, and went out of the shop, without saying another word.

They're rum hogs, some of these mixed breeds, I thought to myself; and walked comfortably up into the city, quite pleasantly aware that a couple of the watching Chinamen were following me. They dropped back, however, near the end of the street, apparently satisfied that I was no one they were looking for.

October 31.

At ten o'clock this morning, I entered Hual Miggett's shop, with a lanky looking "female" upon my arm.

Hual Miggett came forward; and, for a time, the "lady" and I looked at this thing and that, and bought one or two trifles. I observed that the Mixed Breed seemed enormously depressed, and scarcely spoke. He appeared to be pondering something, to the exclusion of everything else. Well, he certainly had enough of troubles to make a man think!

After a few minutes, I beckoned Hual Miggett to take a look up and down the street. Then I told him to see what the big Chinaman was doing. He opened the inner door boldly, and went in, as if to fetch something. When he came back, he told me that the man with the knife was sleeping on the floor.

"Strip off smart now, Billy!" I said to the "woman" I had brought in.

The hat and veil came off instantly, and the very ample dress followed. The result was a typical *seeming* young Chinese, but lean and exceedingly muscular.

"Over there, behind the counter!" I said. "Smart now, before you're seen. Keep your gun handy; but for the Lord's sake don't use it unless you're absolutely cornered."

I had a brace of heavy Colts in my own pockets; for I was taking quite some risks myself, during the next couple of minutes.

"Now, Miggett," I said, "get moving, if you want any of us to come through this with a whole skin. Out with that son of yours!"

I had the dress up, ready in my hands, and Hual Miggett literally dragged the dazed lad out of the mummy-shell. Before he was firmly on his feet, I was pulling the dress over his head. Without waiting to fasten it, I dived for the hat and veil, to get his give-away head and face hidden. In a moment, I had crammed the hat on to him, and dragged the veil over and round his face; then I hurried to fasten the dress. I made my fingers fly! If we had been caught in that minute by the big Chinaman, I should certainly have had to shoot; and then there would have been fifty of the brutes into the shop in no time; and the results would have puzzled our greatest friends to identify; for the beggars have an extraordinary *penchant,* as I might term it, for knife-work.

About a minute later, I was outside the counter again, still with a female-seeming creature upon my arm. A dress and a veil may cover a multitude, well not exactly a multitude; but certainly they make most things look alike!

"Are you ready there, Billy?" I called

softly to the sporting runner, crouching behind the counter.

"Sure," he said.

"Then look out now," I told him. "I'm
going to bring out that big brute. Just let
him see you, and then get away smart; or
there'll be murder done right here. Ready?"

"I guess so," was the confident kind of
answer that pleased me. "The bigger the
guy is the better. It's not him *I'm* botherin'
about; it's the devils in the street."

I turned to the counter, and picked up a
porcelain Mallet vase, which I looked at
with great interest, and suddenly let slip,
with an enormous crash on to the floor,
where it broke into quite some pieces. I
hoped it was valuable. Anyway, it did what
I meant it to do; for the inner door opened
swiftly, and the great bulk of the big Chinaman filled the doorway, as he stared into the
shop.

At the exact instant Billy Johnson, the
runner, glided out from below the end of the
counter nearest to the street, and tip-toed
noiselessly towards the door, in full view of
the big Chinaman.

There was a hideous, inarticulate bull roar from the inner doorway, and I glanced towards the great, flat swaying face. The eyes were glaring, like two greenish slits; and a little froth had blown out over the coarse, walrus-like moustache. There was a crashing of falling gear, as he leaped forward; for he had literally ripped one of the projecting counters clean over on to its side as he made his rush. Then the huge bulk of the great Chinaman dashed past me at a speed that was amazing, considering his size. As he thundered by me, I saw that he had in his hand a great four-foot-long knife. The dull blue glint of the steel shone just for one fraction on my eye; then man and knife were out of the door, with a second crash; for his great shoulder had struck and burst one of the wooden door-posts clean off.

But Billy Johnson was away, thirty yards ahead, running like a deer, with a swift, beautiful, strong pat, pat, pat, of entirely capable feet.

From all sides, as we crowded in the doorway and stared, there were converging upon him ever increasing numbers of Chinamen, seeming to come literally out of nowhere.

The huge Chinaman was still, however, nearer to Johnson than any one else, and running with a grim intentness; his great head held curiously low.

I saw Johnson take the tracks in half a dozen swift steps, and then he was heading straight for the water-side. I heard the sudden, deep, brrp! brrp! of the racing launch's exhaust, distinct above the roar of the growing crowd.

Suddenly the big Chinaman flung up his right hand, and I saw the dull gleam of the yard-long blade.   Then, still running, he threw, and I could not help shouting; though, of course, no one could have heard me in the din that was now going on.

"Missed him!" I yelled; for the big knife had gone slap over Johnson's shoulder, missing him by no more than an inch or two. Evidently the big Chinaman had understood suddenly the plan by which the runner hoped to escape. A number of the other pursuers must also have discovered it on the instant; for there came an irregular ripple of revolver firing; but gun practice is apt to be off the target, when both parties are running.

Then Johnson was at the quay side.

"Safe!" I yelled again, as I saw him jump. "Good man, Johnson! Good man!"

"I guess, Miggett, that's cheap at a thousand dollars," I told him.

There was firing from the dense and increasing bunch of men at the water-side; and from all down the street there was a sound of running feet, as hundreds of American citizens ran up to discover the whereforeness of so much powder and noise.

A City Marshal (a big Irishman by the looks of him) raced up limberly, white-helmeted and superb in summer uniform. I saw him laying about him, cheerfully, on the heads and shoulders (chiefly the heads) of a number of interested and unoffending citizens, who appeared, however, to consider his attentions as the natural order of things.

There was a deal of further gunfiring from the quay front; but already I could see the racing launch, away out in the bay, half a mile or more from the quay.

Up the street, there was a crash of horses' hoofs, as a squad of mounted Marshals swept bang round a corner. They roared down past the shop—big Irishmen, most of them, joyous and holding their guns with a pleasurable expectancy.

"Great sport, Hual Miggett," I said, "over one solitary pigtail!"

The crowd on the water front was fading — literally vanishing; for the mounted Marshals are so inexpressibly and cheerfully effective. And, after all, a bullet fired with a smile . . . almost as one might say, as a jest, is quite as deadly as those dispatched in a more serious spirit.

I glanced at Hual Miggett, and wondered what he was thinking. Possibly quite as much of the yellow god, which had caused all this trouble, as the torpid, cheerless "female" at my side.

"I guess we'd better depart in the confusion," I said. "Come along, sweet maid."

We moved out of the shop, pleasingly unobserved, and reached my ship within the space of two uneventful minutes.

September 1.

We sail to-night, and I went across to see Hual Miggett this morning. I thought that I deserved the reward of virtue; for I had a genuine hankering for that Goat god. But hear the essential meanness of the Mixed Breed.

I found him very glum; but I wasted no pity on him.

"How much for this?" I asked, slapping the Goat god on its capable, bronze shoulder.

"A t'ousand dollars, Cap'n Brother," he said.

"A thousand cents," I answered, and walked towards the door.

"Eight hundred dollars, Cap'n Brother," he called out. "I lose many dollars to you, gladly, for your great goodness to me, Cap'n Brother."

"I don't want you to lose," I said. "We'll drop all talk of what I've done, or haven't done. You're not able to pay me, anyway, even if I'd let you. I'll give you your thousand for the thing, simply because I want it, and I won't have you patting yourself on

that weevily mean back of yours, and thinking you've done *me* a favor. This thing is
worth not a cent more than five or six hundred. Here are the notes. Give me a re-
ceipt, or you'll be swearing I've not paid
you, next. Oh, don't talk. I'm just a bit
sick of you!" I told him.

He tried to excuse himself; but I simply
held out the notes, and waited for the re-
ceipt. Then, without bothering to fall on
his neck and say good-bye, I walked out of
the shop, with the old bronze Goat god
tucked under my arm.

Anyway, I thought to myself, it will be
something to remember this little affair by.

Down in my cabin, however, having
locked the door, I worked the secret opening
in the base of the god, and then, gently and
tenderly, I slid from the hollow interior the
amber god (the Kuch) which I had taken
from the mummy-case, and hidden inside the Goat god, when I sent Hual Miggett for a suit of his son's clothing.

I keep wondering, rather pleasantly, what
the mean-souled Mixture thought, when he
found the yellow god had vanished. Pos-

sibly superstition (being no longer deadened by the drug of Greed) has helped him to some impossible explanation. In any case, he could not very well (after his gorgeous yarn of the President's pigtail) enlarge upon his loss to me. His glumness yesterday and to-day is, perhaps, understandable. The stealing of the amber god cannot have proved a profitable investment of time or labor, not to mention money.

As I look at the wonderful carving of the amber atrocity, I cannot help feeling enormously satisfied with my course of action in this matter. Hual Miggett deserves punishment for a number of undesirable things. Moreover, like Hual Migget, I also know a collector who will pay a good hefty price for the little yellow monster.

CHAPTER IV.

THE RED HERRING

s.s. Calypso,
August 10.

WE docked this morning, and the Customs gave us the very devil of a turn-out; but they found nothing.

"We shall get you, one of these days, Captain Gault," the head of the searchers told me. "We've gone through you pretty carefully; but I'm not satisfied. We've had information that I could swear was sound; but where you've hidden the stuff, I'll confess stumps me out."

"Don't be so infernally ready to give the dog the bad name, and then add insult to injury by trying to hang him," I said. "You know you've never caught me yet trying to shove stuff through."

The head searcher laughed.

"Don't rub it in, Captain," he said. "That's just it! Take the last little flutter of yours, with the pigeons, and the way you made money both ways, both on the hens and on the diamonds; and all the rest of your devil's tricks. You've got the nerve! You ought to be able to retire by now!"

"I'm afraid I'm neither so fortunate nor so clever as you seem to think, Mr. Anderson," I told him. "You had no right to kill my hens, and I made your man apologise for his abominable suggestion about the pigeons!"

"You did so, Cap'n," he said. "But we'll get you yet. And I'll eat my hat if you get a thing through the gates this time, even if we've missed finding it now. We're bound to get you at last. Good-morning, Captain."

"Good-morning, Mr. Anderson," I said. And he went ashore.

There you have the position. I've got £6000 worth of pearls in a remarkable little hiding-place of my own aboard; and somehow word has been passed to the Customs, and it's going to make the getting of them ashore a deuced difficult thing, that will take

some planning. All my old methods, they're
up to. Besides, I never try the same plan
twice, if I can help it; for it is altogether
too risky.

And a lot of them are not half so prac-
ticable as they appear at first. That carrier
pigeon idea, for instance, was both good and
bad; but Mr. Brown and I lost nearly a
thousand pounds' worth of stones through
it; for there's a class of oaf with a gun who
would shoot his own mother-in-law, if she
passed him on wings. Perhaps he'd not be
really to blame in such circumstances; but
he is certainly to blame when he looses off at
a "carrier." Any shooting man should be
able to recognise them from the common or
garden variety. But I fancy the afore-mentioned oaf does the recognising cheerfully,
and shoots promptly. Some of these gentlemen must have made a haul! That was
why we never loosed off the pigeons before reaching port. We never meant to
trust all that value in the air, except as a
last resort.

Anyway, Mr. Anderson and his lot have
got it in for me; and I shall have a job to

get the stuff safely into the right hands by the 20th, which is the date we sail.

August 11.

I have hit on what I believe is rather a smart notion, and I began to develop it to-day.

When I went up to the dock gates this morning, with my bag, I was met by a very courteous and superior person of the Customs Department, who invited me to step into his office. Here, I was again invited into quite a snug little cubicle, and there two searchers made a very thorough examination of me (very thorough indeed!), also of my bag; but, as you may imagine, there was nothing dutiable within a hundred yards of me—that is, nothing of mine.

At the conclusion of the search, after the superior and affable personage had departed, pleasingly apologetic, I was left to acquire clothing and mental equilibrium in almost equal qualities; for I can tell you I was a bit wrathy. And then — perhaps it was just because my mental pot was so a-boil —up simmered *the* idea; and I began straight away on the afore-mentioned developing.

By the time that I had completed my dressing, I had learned not only that the names of the two official searchers were Wentock and Ewiss, but also the numbers of their respective families, and other pleasing details. I dispensed tact and *bonhomie* with liberality, and eventually suggested an adjournment to the place across the road, for a drink.

But my two new (very new) friends shook their heads at this. The "boss" might see them. It would not do. I nodded a complete comprehension. Would they be off duty to-night? They would, at 6.30, prompt.

"Meet me at the corner at seven o'clock," I said. "I've nothing to do and no one to talk to. We'll make an evening of it."

They smiled cheerfully and expansively, and agreed—well, as only such people do agree!

August 18.

The dinner came off, and was in every way a success, both from their point and my point of view. And I think I may say the same of the two dinners that followed on the 15th and the 17th. That was yesterday.

It is now the evening of the 18th, and I'm jotting down what happened, in due order.

It was last night, at our third little dinner together (which for a change I had aboard), that we got really friendly over some of my liqueur whisky. And I saw the chance had come to ask them straight out if they were open to make a fiver each.

The two men looked at each other for a few moments, without speaking.

"Well, Sir, it all depends," said Wentock, the older of the two.

"On what?" I asked.

"We've our place to think of," he said. "It's no use asking us to risk anything, if that's what you mean, Sir."

"There's no risk at all," I told him. "At least, I mean the risk is so infinitesimal as hardly to count at all. What I want you to do, is simply this. To-night, if you agree, I'll hand you over this bag I've got here with me. Take it down to the gates to-mor-

row, and put it somewhere handy in the
office. When I come off from the ship, to
come ashore through the gates, I shall be
carrying another bag, exactly the same as
this in every single detail. You see, I've got
two of them, made exactly alike.

"Well, I shall be stopped, as usual, at the
gates, and taken into the office, and I and
my bag will be pretty well turned inside out
again; which I can tell you I'm getting sick
of, only your people have got it in for me,
pretty savage."

The two searchers grinned at this.

"I ain't surprised, Cap'n," said Wentock,
"with a reputation like yours. Why, they
say as you could retire this minute, with the
brass you've made, running in stuff without
our smelling out the way you do it."

"Don't be so infernally flattering," I told
him. "You mustn't believe half you hear.
And I don't want you to get imagining I do
this kind of thing regularly. It's just a few
trifling trinkets I want to pass in, as a
favor to a friend. Not a habit of mine;
but just once in a way."

Both the men burst into roars of laughter.

They evidently considered this a great joke.

"Well," I said, "let me tell you just what I want you to do.

"When I go into the office, one of you always takes my bag from me. Well, I simply want you to substitute for it the one I shall give you to-night, and which, of course, you can search then as hard as you like, before the Boss. Then, when he goes out hand me back the unsearched one, and I shall just clear off with it, and the trick is done. No risk for you at all. You've simply to take this bag I have here, with a few shore clothes in it, up to the office to-morrow. When I appear, and am searched, you substitute this Number 1 bag for Number 2 which I shall bring in; and you search this Number 1 as fiercely as you like before the Boss. Then, when I am let out, you hand me Number 2, and I go. As for Number 1 I'll make you a present of it, as a little souvenir. Now, say 'yes,' and I'll hand you the fivers now."

Wentock said "yes" promptly for the two of them, and I pulled out my pocketbook, and handed each a five-pound note.

"No," said Wentock quickly. "Gold, if you please, Cap'n. Them things is too easy traced."

I laughed, and passed him across ten sovereigns, and took back my notes.

"You're a smart man, Wentock," I said.

"Have to be, Sir, in our business," he replied, grinning in his cheerfully unscrupulous fashion.

August 19. *a.m.*

I sail to-morrow; so if I don't manage to get the stuff through to-day, I shall be in a hole; for I promised it faithfully, for not later than the 20th.

Later. p.m.

When I took my bag down to the gates to-day to go out, it can be easily imagined that I felt a bit of tension. Six thousand pounds is a lot of risk, apart from the possibility of serious trouble if one is nailed.

However, it had to be done; so I went up to the gates, trying to look as cheerful as usual, and made my accustomed protest against searching, to the genial and diplomatic officer who met me, and invited me to my expected *séance* in the cubicle.

As I was entering the doorway of the outer office, a messenger boy came up to me, and touched his cap.

"Are you Cap'n Gault, Sir?" he asked me.

"I am," I said.

"I just been down to the ship, Sir," he explained. "They said you was just off through the gates, and I might catch you if I hurried. I'm to deliver this letter to you, Sir, and to tell you there ain't no answer. Good-morning, Sir."

"Good-morning,"I said, and tipped him a quarter. Then, as I entered the office with my polite official, I opened the letter.

What I found therein could hardly be supposed to decrease my feelings of tension. The note was printed, crudely, so as to disguise the handwriting. It ran exactly thus—

"Captain Gault,

"s.s. *Calypso*.

"Sir,

"Be advised, and do not attempt to smuggle your stuff through the Customs.

You will be sold if you do, and some one
who cannot help a friendly feeling for you
would regret not to have given you this
chance to draw back. Pay the duty, even
if you lose money. The Authorities know
far more than you can think. They know
absolutely that you bought the 'material'
you wish to smuggle through, and they
know the price you paid, which was £5997.
That is a lot of money to risk losing,
apart from fines and imprisonment. So
be warned and pay the duty in the ordinary
way. I can do no more for you than this.

"A WELLWISHER."

Now, that was what might really be
called a nerve-racker to read, and just after
I had entered the very place that the warning begged me to avoid, at least in what
I might call a "smuggling capacity." I
could not possibly back out now; for suspicion would be inevitable; also my plans
were all arranged.

I went straight on into the place, looking
more comfortable than I felt. I took a
quick look round the inner office, and saw

the end of a bag, half hidden, under a table. That, at any rate, looked as if Ewiss and Wentock meant to be faithful and carry out the substitution, as arranged. If they had given me away, it might be supposed that the bag I had given them would be now in the hands of their superior officers.

I looked at the problem every way. And all the time, as I puzzled, I kept asking myself not only who *wrote* that warning; but who, of all the people I knew, had the necessary *knowledge of detail* that it showed.

Ewiss and Wentock rose from their desks as I entered the private room, and Wentock came forward and took my bag from me, while Ewiss beckoned me towards the cubicle.

The search they made of me was not drastic; but even had it been I should not have minded, in the circumstances. What I was thinking about, all the time, was the bags, and whether the two searchers meant to be faithful to their part of our bargain.

One thing, at first, I placed as an argument in their favor. It was that the unemotional courtesy of the head official was

quite unimpaired; and I could not imagine
that even he would be able to remain so
absolutely and almost statuesquely calm if
my two presumed confederates had given
me away to him, and told him that a big
capture was on the carpet (it was really
linoleum, and cold to the feet!).

There was, however, something disturb-
ing in the attitude of Ewiss. The man
seemed almost hang-doggish, in the way he
avoided meeting my eye. But I could not
say this of Wentock; for that cheerful person was completely his own glad and (as I
always felt) unscrupulous self.

While I was dressing, my bag was
banged down on to the table, and I knew the
instant it was thrown open that Wentock and
Ewiss had sold me; for they had not carried
out the substitution of the Number 1 bag for
the Number 2 which I had just brought in;
but had frankly and brutally ignored our
whole arrangement, and opened Number 2
—the bag that I had bargained with them
should not be opened.

As he flung the bag open, Wentock looked
up at me and grinned broadly. He consid-

ered it evidently a splendid effort of smartness; but it was a faint comfort to my belief in the goodness of human nature that Ewiss looked down at the table and seemed decidedly uncomfortable.

I felt so fierce that I could have given them away, in turn, to their superior for accepting bribes; for it was quite plain now that they had said nothing to him about the plan I had proposed to them to substitute one bag for the other. I could see their way of looking at the whole business. They were not readily bribable; but if people were foolish enough to offer them a bribe it was accepted—as a *present;* and so much the worse for the person who offered it, and so much the better for the officer presented with this kind of—shall I say "honorarium"! I think any one must admit I had cause to feel bitter.

I did not, of course, think really of giving them away; for there might have been a charge made of bribery and corruption; whilst they, as I was pretty sure, would say nothing, lest they be mulcted of the "presents" I had made them; and also, possibly, have a reprimand for meddling with my proposition in any way at all.

The search Wentock gave that bag was a revelation of drastic thoroughness. I remonstrated once, and said I would put in a claim for a new bag; for Wentock, as he went further and further, and found nothing, seemed almost inclined to rip the bag to pieces, so sure was he that he "had me safe."

At last, he had to give it up, and pronounced it free of all dutiable stuff, which of course it was; for, as I told him later, I had considered the chances of their proving treacherous, and had carefully omitted on this occasion to put anything dutiable into the bag. I told them that it must be regarded as a kind of trial trip, to test their intentions.

This was as soon as the Boss had left the cubicle; and then I cut loose on the two of them.

"For a couple of treacherous, grunting human hogs, you two are something to talk about!" I told them. "You take my money with one hand, and try to do me in with the other. Suppose you hand out that cash I gave you!"

Wentock laughed outright at this, as if it were a particularly nutty kind of joke; but I was glad to see that Ewiss looked more uncomfortable than ever.

"Our perquisites, Cap'n," said Wentock. "We're often asked out to a bit of dinner, and we get people who are mighty anxious to hand us nice little cash presents, *ad lib.,* as you might say, every once in a while. And we don't say 'no,' do we, Ewiss? Seeing we're both married men, with families to bring up, and remembering, Cap'n, how affectionate you've asked after the youngsters, you might remember us again, Cap'n, when you've any odd cash as you don't want burning holes in your pocket. Likewise we both admired them dinners you stood us up town. You can do it again, Cap'n, any time you like, and keep on doing it. We're always open. If you can stand it, we can. Now, how would to-night suit you? We're both free and——"

"Go to blazes!" I said, "and stay there. You're a pair of treacherous animals, like all your kind, and you might have ruined me, if I hadn't been careful. Give me my bags, and be damned to you! They say never trust a policeman, even if he's your own brother. He'll lock you up first chance he gets for the sake of promotion. And I guess you're the same kind of cheap stuff."

And with that I picked up my bags and walked out, Wentock holding the door for me. But Ewiss was looking as thoroughly miserable and ashamed as a man need look.

"How would to-night suit you, Sir?" called Wentock after me as I passed through the gates.

"Go to the devil!" I said. "And get him to shut your infernal mouth with a red-hot brick."

And with that I boarded a street car and went rather thoughtfully up town.

August 19. *Later still.*

As it chances, I have invited the men to dinner again — both of them; for I'm not the kind of man who likes taking a fall too quietly.

This is what I wrote, addressing it to Wentock at the office—

"DEAR MR. WENTOCK,

"I have been thinking things over a bit, and have come to the conclusion that everything was not said at our last meeting that might have been said. I bear no malice at all for the somewhat pungent wit you handed out to me. I guess I was in the position that invited a few jabs.

"I have been thinking that perhaps there is still a way to arrange this affair a little more to my liking, and I can assure you and your friend that you will be the gainers, and without having your strict feelings for high honesty and fairness outraged.

"Will you both meet me at our little restaurant to-night at the usual time, and I will go thoroughly into the matter; for as I start off to-morrow, it is imperative to me to carry through my plan before I sail.

"Remember, I bear no malice at all. Look upon this as an entirely business-like and reasonable friendly little invite.

"Yours sincerely,

"G. GAULT."

I sent this by messenger, and to-night I shall be at the restaurant.

August 20.

They both came to time.   Wentock as cheerful and unscrupulous as ever.   Ewiss, looking awkward, and as if he would rather have stopped away.

"Now," I said as we sat down, "pleasure first and business afterwards."   And I reached for the hock.

"One moment, Sir," said Ewiss, suddenly, and pushed forward a small roll of paper, which I took from him, feeling a little puzzled.

It contained dollar notes to the approximate value of five pounds.   I looked across at Ewiss with sudden gladness and respect in my heart; for I understood.   But what I said was—

"What are these, Mr. Ewiss?"

"It's your brass, Cap'n," he said.   "I've thought a deal lately, an' I reckon I can't hold on to it.   I'm not grumbling at Mr. Wentock's way of looking at it.   Lots of our men look at it that way; but even if you'd no right to try to bribe me, that doesn't say as I'm right to take your brass, an' mean to sell you all the time.   If I'm above the job you wanted me to do, I feel I ought to be above taking the brass for it, too. So take it back, Sir; an' after that I shall enjoy my dinner with you as well as any one."

I looked across at Wentock.

"And you?" I asked.

"Well," he said, grinning in his cheerful fashion, "I don't see it that way, Cap'n. Ewiss, here, always was a bit funny on that point. Sometimes I've screwed him up to our general way of looking at it; but, in the main, he's not built on those lines, and I don't grumble at him any more than he don't grumble at me. I look at it this way. You, or any man as insults me by tryin' to buy me, has got to pay for it."

"Good man, Wentock," I said. "It takes a deal of different opinions to oil the different kinds of consciences. I've a brand of my own, and you've a brand of your own, and Mr. Ewiss, there, has his. Anyway, you're welcome to the cash, Mr. Wentock. As for you, Mr. Ewiss, I see you can't take yours; so I'll have it back, and I apologise to you. I think your way is the soundest of the three of us. Now, forgetting all this, let's drop the serious for a time, and we'll have our dinner."

*　　*　　*　　*

It was over the wine that I explained to Wentock the things I had to explain. Ewiss was out of it, though he listened quietly, with the deepest interest, and a flash of a smile now and again that showed he had a sense of humor.

"You see, Wentock," I said, "I never meant to bribe either of you, but only to make you *think* that I did. No man in his senses would risk £6,000 — to be exact, £5,997" (I glanced at Ewiss and smiled; for I had guessed who was my "well-wisher") —"on a piffly little bribe like a couple of fivers. If I had seriously meant to buy you, I should have offered something nearer your price, say fifty or a hundred pounds. As it was, I wanted merely, by means of my trifling bribes, to make you think I was going to run the stuff through in the way I explained so carefully. In other words, I wished to focus your entire suspicions upon Number 2 bag, thereby insuring that the Number 1 bag, which I left in your hands,

should receive only the most casual attention; for you would, naturally, taking my
plan at its face value, think only of the second bag, which I assured you I did not want
searched. Moreover, it would seem self-
evident to you that the Number 1 bag,
which I handed entirely over to your care,
would never have anything dutiable in it;
for, had you acted up to your agreement,
there was no apparent reason for supposing
that I would ever even handle it again. To
insure your subconsciously realizing this, I
even told you you could keep it, once it had
served me in the matter of the substitution.

"Of course, had you been faithful to our
arrangement and substituted the Number 1
bag, to be searched, for the Number 2 bag,
which I brought with me, I might have been
in a hole. You see, the handle of the Number 1 bag contained the particular, shall we
say, trinkets you were anxious to lay
hands on.

"But then, I knew, both from the small-
ness of my bribe and from my reading of
your face, and from the ways of Customs
officials in general, that you would go for

the big 'cop' you felt sure you were wise to. It might have meant promotion—oh, and quite a number of desirable things, from your point of view.

"After all, Wentock, even you," I said quietly and pleasantly, "will agree that Honesty's best Policy!

"And that concludes all I have to say, practically. I planned it all out, even to the burst of anger and the snatching up of both my bags and walking off in that quite superb indignation, on discovery of your treachery. I did it well, didn't I?—while you were so pleasingly and wittily inviting yourself to this final little dinner, which I had, even then, planned, like all the rest of it.

"As I said in my note, you would be the gainers for coming to-night. That is so; for you are the richer for a dinner and an explanation, and Mr. Ewiss for an apology. That is all."

CHAPTER V

THE DRUM OF SACCHARINE

S.S. Adriatic,
May 23.

MR. ARMES, my First Mate, and Mr. James, the Second, had a row to-day. They clubbed together in port and bought a hundred pounds of saccharine.

The duty on it, going into England, is considerable — sevenpence an ounce, upwards. In this case the duty will amount to about fifteen shillings a pound, as the stuff is over "proof," as I might say, and the duty varies according to strength. I think the two of them are rather aghast at their own daring; they've been planning, all the way home, how they're going to get the "goods" through the Customs.

Mr. Armes mentioned to me the proposition he and the Second Mate had in mind. This was after they'd bought the stuff, and I

told him it would not interfere with anything I was doing, and they could go ahead.
Only, if the Customs dropped on the saccharine, they must own up and pay the fine
themselves. For I was not going to have the
ship fined.

This was on the bridge, and he grinned at
me, warningly.

"Sst! Remember the man at the wheel,
Sir!" he said.

The row they had to-day came about
through Mr. Armes proposing to hide the
stuff in a big, empty paint-drum, which was
to be made water-tight and then lowered
over the side before the searchers came
aboard. They would sink it on the end of
a line and buoy the end with a casual bit
of cork. Then, when the search was over,
they would only have to get hold of the in-
conspicuous little float and haul the stuff up
again.

The Second Mate's notion was to hang the
stuff down inside the hollow steel mainmast
with a thin wire, the end of which could
be fixed by jamming it under one of the
nuts that held down the lid that covers the

top of every mast that isn't a spike mast.

It was in this morning's watch that they got rowing about the thing—each wanting his own way and each sure that his method of hiding the stuff was the best.

Finally, they came up to me to ask my opinion. I was on the bridge at the time, and I had to keep telling them to speak quieter; for I could see that Sedwell, the man at the wheel, was curious.

When my two officers had explained their ideas I told them how I felt in the matter. I said that, possibly, the Second Mate's plan was quite as good as the Mate's; but it was no better, and certainly not as safe; for if the stuff were found outside the ship neither they nor the ship could be fined, as long as there were no witnesses, and they would lose only the price they had paid for the stuff— though, of course, this would be bad enough; for the two of them had spent a year's savings on their "speculation."

But I made it clear to them that I left the choice entirely with them. I preferred the First Mate's method, chiefly because it would keep the ship free; and I fancy we want to let things rest a bit; for I can tell lately, by the thoroughness of the official search, after each voyage, that we are somewhat under a cloud! Perhaps we have deserved it; for certainly I've had some very good luck lately.

"But, mind you," I said, "I stand out of this business altogether. Do it your own way, and, profit or loss, you must take the responsibility. I merely advise the two of you to take the First Mate's plan of sinking the stuff to a small float alongside just before the searchers come aboard. . . ."

"Sshh, Sir! Not too loud!" said Mr. James, the Second Mate, holding up his hand, quickly.

I stopped at once; for I had certainly spoken a little louder, in my intention to make it clear that I stood entirely out of the business, lock, stock and barrel, as you might say.

I glanced over at Sedwell, at the wheel. It struck me that the man was plainly trying to hear what we were saying, and I stepped over quickly to look at the compass. I found that he had indeed been taking more notice of the two officers' argument than of his steering; for the vessel was nearly two points off her course. I suggested to Sedwell that our ideas of steering were not, perhaps, quite identical. I endeavored to fuse this suggestion into him in as few words as possible, and returned to where the two Mates were standing.

"He was certainly trying to hear," I told them; "but I'm pretty sure he's heard nothing that matters. In fact, I'm *sure* he's heard nothing that could give your plans away."

"So are we, Sir," said the Second Mate, Mr. James. "We both tried to catch the few carefully chosen phrases you dealt out to him" (they both grinned) ; "but we could only just hear the more vigorous portion!"

May 24.

We docked this evening, and I was certainly interested to see whether the two of them got the stuff through; for a hundred pounds of saccharine is a hefty quantity to try to smuggle casually into port and afterwards ashore through the officers at the dock gates.

Apparently, the First Mate's plan was the one they'd chosen, for they disappeared below with the biggest empty paint-drum we've got in the ship. I stayed on the bridge all the morning, so as to give them full liberty; and they fixed and caulked the thing up in my cabin, where no one could see them.

Just before the officers came aboard, the Mate slipped away aft, to where he had previously slung the paint-drum over the quarter. He took a look round, then lowered it rapidly away, and let go the end of the line, to which he had bent on a piece of rough cork, that looked as if it were nothing but a bit of old stuff that was just floating about in the water.

It was Sedwell's wheel again, as it chanced; and when I turned from having a quick look to see how the Mate had managed I caught Sedwell also staring aft, over his shoulder, at the Mate.

I explained to Sedwell that, as a variant, he might as well take a look ahead, now and then, to see that we made some show of following in the wake of the tug.

When the Customs came up over the side, we were already a hundred feet ahead of the place where the Mate had let go the buoyed paint-drum; and I felt that the thing should succeed; for we were going slowly ahead all the time.

Yet, I was a little anxious about Sedwell, in one or two ways. The man plainly had some suspicion; but as we moved steadily farther and farther away, I felt safer about the saccharine.

It would be impossible for him to get away from the ship before dark. I could see to that! And then, he could do no harm; for the two Mates would have had ample time, by then, to deal with the stuff themselves.

The officers reported themselves to me; but before we went down into the cabin, to go through the usual preliminaries, I excused myself a moment and had a word with Mr. Armes.

"That man, Sedwell, is on to the game," I told him. "Watch him."

"Very good," said the Mate, "I'll certainly watch him, Sir!"

Down in my cabin, the officers struck me as being most perfunctory in their work. I asked them to take a look through my gear, as I wanted to get ashore as soon as possible. Here again, their attitude was most peculiar. Instead of the exact and elaborate search-methods that have been lately wasted on my ship, they simply made believe to look over my belongings, and were actually out of the cabin within five minutes.

This made me form certain conclusions, and when I went up on deck again I had word with my two officers.

"They've done my place already," I told them. "Hardly looked at a thing!"

"Same with us, Sir," said the two Mates. "Looks as if we were getting to be considered a reformed character, as one might say."

"Rather rich, after the way you cleared all that stuff safely last trip, Sir!" said Mr. James, my Second.

The two of them grinned at me; but I pulled them up.

"You'll grin on the other side," I told

them "if this business of yours goes wrong! Have you kept an eye on that Sedwell?"

"Yes, Sir," said the First Mate.

"Excuse me, Sir, shoving in cheeky like," said the bo'sun, coming up to me at this moment; "but I been watchin' that Sedwell. I knows as you got a little flutter on wiv' the Custom people, an' I sees the Mate dump the stuff astern; an' then I sees that yon Sedwell 'ad seen it, same as me. Well, I didn't know as it mattered, till the search officers come up on the bridge to see you, Sir, an' you goes down to speak to the First Mate. But then I got suspicious; for I seen the officers swappin' quick talk with Sedwell, quiet like; and then, when you went up again on the bridge, they made as if they'd never seen 'im. An' now, look at 'em, they ain't more than pretendin' to search the ship. I 'ope you don't mind my shoving in like this, Sir; but I'd lay my pay-day to a marlin-spike, as yon Sedwell's split."

"Thank you, Bo'sun," I said. "I'll remember this. Keep an eye on Sedwell while you're about the deck."

As the bo'sun walked away, I looked at

the two Mates, and the two Mates looked at me.

"This will need some pondering about," I said, gravely.

"What do you think they will do?" asked Mr. Armes. And the two of them stared at me.

"Exactly what you'd expect them to do," I said. "They'll send out a boat to find the buoy. They'll set a watch then, until you go for the stuff. Then they'll arrest you, and there'll be something more than the usual bother. You see, it's a reasonable little haul is a hundred pounds of saccharine; though what'll make them hot will be to nab us for our past flutters. I should leave it strictly alone. They can't possibly *prove* anything against you; for there's no mark on the paint-drum that Sedwell can swear to; and unless they catch you in the act of hauling it up, you can just keep mum and smile at them. Of course, you'll have to lose all that valuable stuff!"

The two Mates grinned at me in what, by a suspicious onlooker, might have been considered a sickly fashion.

"It's better, anyway, than anything else you can do," I said, "except come up to the hotel to-night, and I'll stand you both a good dinner to cheer you up."

They both agreed that I was right and accepted my invitation. After all, there was no other course for them to steer.

A little later, a shore-boat signalled us ahead and hooked on alongside as we came up. A messenger boy had brought an express letter from the owners, asking me to go ashore at once on important business. As I was reading it, the Chief of the Customs came up to see me, before going ashore, and I had to have a few words with him.

He and his men had certainly done their work in record time. It was quite plain to me that the "A.B." Sedwell was a Customs spy, who had shipped for the voyage out and home with us, to try to get a case against the ship or the officers. This is sometimes done (though never admitted) where the authorities have begun to be suspicious of smuggling in a particular vessel, yet cannot fix any proof on her.

"Perhaps you won't mind putting me ashore in your launch?" I asked the Chief, as he shook hands. "The owners want to see me at once."

He agreed cordially, and I shouted to the steward to bring out my portmanteaux, which he had just been packing.

"I'll leave you to see her made fast, Mister," I called to the First Mate. "As soon as I've done my business, I shall take rooms at the *Gwalia*."

This was to let him know where to pick me up before going out to the dinner I had promised him and the Second Mate.

Twenty minutes later I was ashore. I shared a taxi, part of the way up from the docks, with our genial but dangerous enemy, the Chief of the search officers. As I dropped him, I could not help wondering whether their boat had already gone out to find the buoyed saccharine.

It is strange, this almost amicable cut-and-thrust, that is none the less deadly because of the quietness and courtesy with which the thrust may be given. Here was I, seated in a taxi, sharing it with the well and pleasant mannered man on the seat alongside of me, who would, on the first opportunity, do his best to get me into serious trouble, even as I have undoubtedly got him certain ratings from his superiors in office, owing to my wits having, up to the present, out-matched his, as he and they know very well, but cannot prove.

I thought his eyes twinkled over some secret thought, as he jumped down and shook hands. No doubt he anticipated that the lure of the sunk saccharine would be bound to bring us straight into his hands that very night.

Maybe my own eyes twinkled as I said good-bye. He might watch a long time, so far, at least, as I was concerned, before the big, sunk paint-drum had a visitor. If only he knew just how much I knew! I thought to myself as I sat back, smiling.

Then I lapsed into serious thought — a hundred pounds of saccharine represents a certain amount of money. It was a lot for my two Mates to have staked on a single throw of the Customs dice, as one might say.

Well! Well! . . . I turned my thoughts on a space, to dinner. At least, I could promise that it should be made a cheering function.

*   *   *   *

We had dinner in a private room at the *Cecil*.

"Certainly, Mr. Armes and Mr. James," I told them, as I handed them a fat little bank-note each, "the occasion demands joy, and I think this slight celebration is almost morally justified."

My two officers smiled at me, and I raised my glass.

"Here's my toast," I said—

" 'To the flour that lies in the paint-drum,
    To the spy that we spotted at once,
    To the two portmanteaux that carried the stuff
    While the Customs swallowed our jolly good bluff
    That we worked on the dunce,
    Viz. Sedwell the bum—
A right proper bum of a Customs House watcher,
Who heard, ah! I fear,
What he has wanted to hear,
Just that, and no more!
Let us drink to the dear!' "

I had put this into shape while I was sitting waiting for them; and, really, I think it explains all that there is to explain.

We all drank; and as we drank, I doubt not, that, out on the dark waters of the river, a number of Customs officials kept a shivery and lurid watch for the smugglers who came not.

CHAPTER VI

THE PROBLEM OF THE PEARLS

S.S. Zurich,
June 17.

"IF I'd only had sense to stay ashore when I was a boy and play the fiddle or the flute, I'd have made my fortune," I told Mister Gamp, my First Mate, this morning.

Gamp's got the morals of a virago and the tongue of an Irishman. Oh, I mean it that way! If a virago were moral, she'd hold her tongue and stop being a virago; and if an Irishman held his tongue, he'd stop being an Irishman; so there you are! Any way, Gamp wasn't complimentary; but he granted it helped a man to think; and somehow the way he admitted even that much wasn't nice.

We're away and away-o across the Western Ocean, bound for little old New York; and I fiddle and flute a bit, as you might say, to keep my hand in, and likewise to help me think.

You see, I've cause to think. I undertook a little private contract, when we were in Amsterdam. I bought six pearls for the respectable sum of £12,375 from a merchant I know there. I supplied the judgment, and a friend of mine, in the jewel trade in New York, supplied the cash. My job now is to hand these over to my friend in New York, without undergoing the, shall we call it, formalities, of paying the ridiculous duty which the Customs attempt to enforce?

Unfortunately, I am not unknown to the New York Customs; though, with my hand on my heart, I assure you there has never been anything so vulgar as a, shall I say, *débâcle* on my part? During the last few years, I have turned an honest dollar or two in this pretty game of wits wit who can; but there! Why give way to naughty vanity? It comes too often before the aforementioned *débâcle* to be a safe vice for a jewel runner.

Now, because of past episodes with the people across the way (I refer to the New

York Customs) I have been subjected to flattering attentions from their agents, who keep an unobtrusive eye upon the jewel marts of Amsterdam and other places, with or without dams, where the precious "pills" and "pebbles" are on sale.

Because of this *espionnage* (a most suitable and fashionable phrase!) I took particular care to "arrange" my transaction with the merchant in Amsterdam. I 'phoned him from a public cabaret; and only when I had him on the wire did I give my name, and such other particulars are were necessary. I told him to meet me on the Dam, on the Palace side, away from the cafés.

I drove round to the back of the Palace, in a taxi, and told the driver to wait, while I had a walk on to the big square. Here I found my business acquaintance, and took him back to my taxi, and told the man to drive out to the model cheese farms.

"You indrested mit cheese, Cap'n?" asked my acquaintance, smiling.

"Nix!" I told him, in the vernacular. "I want to get away from the cafés. We've not got to be seen together. When we get out there, I'll leave you in the taxi and come back by tram. I guess you'll have to pay the taxi. If I'm.seen with you, there'll go a message to New York, and they'll be waiting for me with open arms, as you might say. . . . I'd have the very devil then to get the stuff through."

He nodded; and we turned to business.

When we reached the cheese farms, we had done business to the tune of the aforementioned £12,375; and I had paid him in cold cash. In return, I had six really wonderful pearls; and the whole transaction was finished.

"I'm off, now," I said, and stopped the cabby. "I think we're safe; but it's better to part here."

"Shoost so," he agreed, and I jumped out.

"Back to the Dam," I told the driver, and stood away, while he turned, feeling thankful that I had managed the thing so neatly.

And then, just as the driver let in his clutch again, the ass of a merchant shoved his fat, round face out of the taxi—

"Goot voyage, Cap'n!" he said, beaming like a blooming full moon. "Und I pe glad to know you get all safe trou de Gusdoms."

"Shove your head in, you idiot!" I said. "Quick!"

He looked startled, and his face went back into the taxi, with considerable speed, for so fat a man. I saw the vehicle lurch as he sat down; and then it gathered way and presently vanished in the distance.

I turned round from watching it, and pulled out a cigarette. As I did so, I saw a man step back rather hastily, into one of the small village shops, a little way up the short street. There was something at once familiar and suspicious about the thing I had seen. Why should a man seem to dodge back into one of the shops? And why had I that vague sense of something familiar?

I walked up to the door of the shop, one of those Dutch shops that seem to overflow innumerable broods of brass candlesticks, unnamable pottery and unashamedly "antique" furniture, lying in wait to pounce upon the expectedly asinine tourist.

I went right into the shop, and stared, for maybe a full minute, at a back that I seemed to know. It was *very* "touristy," in the worst "British" style, by means of which Continental tailors vent upon Britain the venom of centuries. But I was sure that I knew what I might call "the Man in the Checked Coat" — and trousers, of course; not to forget the stockings that would have put to shame a full-blooded Cockney.

I was sure the man's interest in the impossible plaque he was studying was due to the fact that it offered so good an excuse to withdraw from me the light of his countenance.

But I persisted in my exposition of patience; and because I stood so calmly behind him, the woman in the shop did not press me to buy a fumed-oak cradle for the babe that I have not; being evidently under the impression that I was a friend of the man in the checked coat, and was no more than waiting for him—which was a just and exact estimate of what I was doing.

At last, the plaque afforded no longer any pretext for silence and study; and the man, evidently embarrassed, unhung it, and presented it to the woman, with a dumb gesture of: "How much?"

"Twenty florins?" said the woman, without changing color.

The unfortunate man paid the money, grabbed the plaque, and walked out hastily, tumbling over a cradle and upsetting half a dozen Birmingham candlesticks, in his anxiety to go out with his back turned to me, and yet to appear as if he were not badly deformed or mentally deficient.

But I knew who it was; for I had got one good, square look at his side face. It was James Atkinson, one of the most active of the Customs' agents on the European side of the pond.

And now, as I fiddle and flute, here in my chart-house, I am eternally asking myself: Did he see *who* I was with, in the taxi? That's the question! If he did, then good-bye to my getting the pearls ashore, without the devil's own trouble!

I know the New York Customs! They're IT—when it comes to acting on sure information! They'll turn the ship inside out, and afterwards skin her alive, before they'll let these six wee jewels of the sea get past their infernal hawks'-eyes! Gracious me!

I wish I knew! How I wish I knew!

Do you wonder that I fiddle and flute, flute and fiddle, and that Mr. Gamp looks sourer and sourer, and wears ostentatious pads of cotton wool in his somewhat over-sized ears? I'm sure I don't blame him. It's as absurd to blame a man for having no soul for music, as it is to blame a man for being born without legs? You don't *blame* him?

Meanwhile, what *did* that infernal Atkinson-Paul-pry see or suspect?

New York, June 29.

"I'd like a word with you in the cabin, Captain Gault."

Those were the words I got from Mac-Allister, the Chief searcher, when he came aboard this morning, as we were docking. I knew then that the agent in Amsterdam *had* seen who was in the taxi; and if he had seen that much, there was a good certainty he'd followed up the clue. . . . Well, it was no use cursing; so I went below with the searcher.

"Look here, old man," he said, in his

friendly way, when we reached the cabin, "we *know* you've got pearls. We know you paid £12,375 for six of them. Is that enough to show you it's no use playing tricks and getting yourself into trouble? Be a sensible man and *don't* try to run 'em through. You can't do it; for we're alive to what you're up to.

"Now, I've warned you fair!" he went on; "so you're getting a square chance. I ask you now, formally, Captain Gault, have you anything to declare?"

"Nothing, dear man," I said.

"I'm sorry," he replied. "I've given you every chance, and now I tell you plainly that if the Boss can nail you, he'll do it, and he'll not spare you, either. You've had things too much your own way, and you think you can't get caught. Now, you'll see!"

"Excuse me one moment, Mac," I said. "But I thought I heard some one outside the door."

I stepped across smartly, as I spoke, and slammed it open; but there was no one there.

"Funny!" I said, "I could have sworn I heard something."

"So could I," said MacAllister, looking puzzled. "Any way, there's no one; and I guess now I'd better get up and put my men on to the job of rooting out where you've hid the pills. You're an owl, old man, to butt into trouble like this!"

New York, July 3.

Well, that was something of a search! Though I wasn't afraid they'd ever find the place where I've hid the stuff. They'd have to take the ship to pieces, first; but they did their best! They kept thirty men on the job, for seventy-two hours, changing them every eight hours. They simply mapped the vessel out into sections, and went over every available foot of her; but there are many unavailable feet in a vessel; and six pearls can lie in a very small space indeed. I need hardly add that they searched me also, and my personal belongings. They found nothing.

They searched everybody and everything that came near the ship, so it seemed to me, also they've got one of their men aboard all the time, to keep a general eye on things. The final trouble was a pompous Treasury official, who came down and tried to bully me—

"We know you've got the pearls," he told me. "We know it, because we know all about you, and all you did in Amsterdam. You bought six pearls from Van Lumb, and you paid £12,375 for them. That means that somewhere in this ship there are hidden over sixty thousand dollars' worth of pearls. And we mean to have them. Where are they?"

."Now, Sir," I said, "you've asked me a leading question, and I'll answer it as frankly as it was asked. I'm a bit of a ladies' man, like I've heard say you are yourself, when your wife's gone South.

"Well, I guess you'll feel in sympathy with me when I tell you I bought those pearls for a lady friend of mine, and she's got them this present moment."

"Don't talk nonsense," he said, getting warm. "Your ship sailed direct here from Amsterdam. You were watched every hour in Holland, after you bought the pearls."

"It was since then," I explained. "My dear man, do be a bit more helpful. These —er—affairs are somewhat delicate to talk about, as you should know; but I suppose I had better forget my finer feelings. In short, Sir, the lady was one we met on the trip across."

"What!" he said. "You have neither touched anywhere nor boarded any vessel since leaving the Continent of Europe. What do you mean by this stupidity? There are no ladies floating loose about on the North Atlantic!"

"Well, you see," I continued, "I was not right in calling her a lady — as a matter of honest fact she was only a mere maid— er—I believe it is fashionable to omit the second 'e'!"

He got up then, and went. I've seen him since; and I've felt him, often, or rather the effects of him, for the way I'm searched each time I go ashore is nothing short of immodest.

The first time I went ashore I was stopped by the Customs, and taken into a comfortable enough office, with a room at the back of it that I know too well by now, for I've been there before. It has a big skylight overhead, plus windows all round, except where a cubicle stands in one corner.

There were two officers in the place, and I was invited to step into the cubicle and strip. The two officers then took my clothes out into the room and examined every square inch of them, also my boots; they were very particular about the heels; but they found everything all right. Then they started on me, and gave me a similar course of treatment. It was very embarrassing; but life has its thorny places; so I made the best of things.

They found nothing, of course, for I wasn't risking sixty thousand dollars, odd, on the chance of getting through, unsearched. After they had searched me, they examined the floor and walls of the cubicle, to be sure I had not dropped anything, or stuck anything up above the eye "level" with a bit of chewing gum. They were up to all the dodges!

Then they introduced me to a new fakement, an upright grey panel, that I had to stand against, with a pattern of big brass balls, on a framework, the other side of me. They pulled a switch and flared off a criss-cross of great violet colored sparks, that went jumping and cracking across and across the curious framework of brass balls.

I saw then that they were trying some kind of X-ray test on me. They repeated this, elaborately; then told me I might dress.

When I was finished I went out into the big, well-lighted room, and here I found the two officers, with MacAllister and a man with an apron on and bare-armed, who I supposed might be a photographer. They were all examining a number of big, oblong pieces of paper, which I saw must be some kind of paper negative. It was most extraordinary to see the hidden parts of my own anatomy brazening their shadows there for every one of their callous eyes to examine.

MacAllister, the Chief searcher, turned to me.

"Sorry, Captain Gault, to have put you

through it like this," he said, speaking a little formally before the three men. "But we know you've got those pearls, and I guess we're going to have them. You've only yourself to thank for putting us to all this trouble. I assure you, we ain't keen on it! But it's what you're liable to get each time you come ashore. And it's what any one else is liable to get, if we see anything that looks like your trying to use any one else to put the pills past us."

"Any further operations, or may I go now?" I asked. "You certainly are the limit on this side of the pond!"

"As I've said, Captain Gault, I'm sorry; but you've brought it on yourself," he replied, as friendly as ever. "We *know* you've diddled the U.S.A. Customs to the tune of thousands, only we've not been able to *prove* it yet. You've put it over on us that much we'll be getting superstitious if we don't hand you out a take-down before long. Why, man, you're the swellest Contrabandist this side of Jerusalem!"

"You've no right to make such a statement!" I said. "If you care to come outside and say a thing of that sort before witnesses who aren't your own men, I'll have a writ on you for libel before forty-eight hours are out."

MacAllister laughed.

"I don't doubt it, Captain Gault," he said. "In fact, I'm sure of it. You're the Wonder Unlimited! The way you put it over us with that cigarful of pearls last trip—— Well!"

"Look here!" I warned him. "That's a proved libel; so be careful. I won my case against the Treasury on that same statement, and they had to bail up on it——"

The Chief searcher roared.

"I know it, old man," he called out, shaking all over, and forgetting any attempt at formality in his exuberance. "All little old New York knows it. . . . You're *the* Classic!"

Everybody in the room appeared to be laughing, and I laughed with them. Then, in the midst of our laughter, a voice spoke from the doorway leading out into the office—

"What's the meaning of this? Mr. Mac-

Allister, are you making free with that smuggling scoundrel there?"

I recognised the voice, even as I turned. It was the Treasury official who had been vanquished by my tale of the mere maid who wasn't a lady.

I glanced at MacAllister, and saw that he was annoyed at his superior's manner. The two other officers and the photographer looked as if they had never laughed in their lives. They bent, all of them, over the paper negatives, and it was I who answered His Mightiness.

"Were you referring to me, Sir?" I asked him.

"I have no wish to bandy words with you!" he said, speaking like a "comic" Englishman out of an American "best-seller." He turned to MacAllister again—

"Have you searched this person?" he asked the Chief searcher.

"Sure," said MacAllister, tersely. "If it's Captain Gault you mean." He looked at me—

"I guess you can pass out, Sir," he said, and nodded towards the doorway.

· "Thanks," I replied. "Good-morning."

At the doorway, however, the uncivil personage from the Treasury forgot his commendable intention not to speak to me.

"Look here, you—you smuggling scamp," he said. "I've given orders that you're to be searched every time you come ashore. We shall have those pearls, never fear! We shall have them. You will never bring them ashore past *my* men!" He stamped his foot. "We shall catch you before many days are past; and I will see that you suffer bitterly—bitterly. You are an unmitigated, thieving scoundrel. You are a——"

"Ah!" I said, blandly interrupting him. "Let me see your tongue." I slipped my forefinger under his scraggy and dyspeptic chin and tilted his face up gently but firmly. "Ah!" I said. "I thought so! Your eyes tell a sad tale, my dear Sir. Liver! Undoubtedly liver! Try a course of Epsoms, my dear Sir. Magnificent thing, Epsoms. A sure tonic, Sir. You will hardly recognise yourself afterwards. Your friends certainly won't. A great improver of a coarse complexion and coarse manners, Sir. Try it."

And with the last word I took my finger from under the little man's chin and passed out. As I went I thought the dead silence of the inner room was broken by sounds that suggested the kind of agony men feel who stifle a large and natural laughter.

July 5.

I invited MacAllister aboard last night, to have a smoke and a yarn with me. As I·pointed out to him, I could not be getting into mischief if he were with me, and I wanted some one to talk to. I told him, also, there was something I wanted to speak to him about, whereat I believe he scented regeneration! Also, I added that he could have some music, if he liked. And here, let me say, that my fiddling and fluting is not quite so bad as Mr. Gamp's attitude might suggest to a stranger.

MacAllister agreed, and we had a very pleasant evening. He plays the fiddle a bit, and I accompanied him with the flute. Between whiles, we smoked and yarned; and it was understood that, for that one evening, pearls were strictly taboo.

However, just when he was leaving, I

made the protest that had been in my mind all evening.

"Look here, dear man," I said. "I don't think it's the thing for the man you've put aboard to keep an eye on things, to go round on a private search-stunt of his own, among my personal belongings. If he wants to search my gear, I'm reasonably willing, at any reasonable time, provided I'm present; but it's bad cricket doing that sort of thing when I'm ashore!"

MacAllister was simply astonished, genuinely; but he asked me to send Pelter, my Steward, for the man at once.

When he came, MacAllister turned on him and asked what the deuce he meant by exceeding instructions. But the man swore he had done nothing more than keep a general eye on things. He had never once been into my cabin, except during the time of the search of the vessel. He stuck to this statement, and, at last, MacAllister sent him away.

"Are you sure?" he asked me. "What makes you sure there's been any one among your gear?"

"Things disarranged; one lock forced and another jammed through some one tackling it too roughly with a key that didn't fit!" I told him.

He nodded.

"Proof enough, old man!" he said. "I'm puzzled. Yet I'm inclined to believe our man, Quill. He's a straight one, or we shouldn't have put him on to this job. What about your man, Pelter, the Steward? He may be looking out for the pills himself. However, that's your look out!

"I guess, anyway, he knows he's on to a safe thing, if it's him. You see, if he gets them from you, you daren't put the police on him; for then we'd drop on you for the duty, and we'd confiscate the pearls as well, even if the police got them back from Pelter. No! I guess you're in a corner, if he or any one else can put a finger on them.

"As a friend, I should advise you to keep your eyes skinned. As a Customs official, I say it'll serve you right if you get done.

"Now let's drop the subject. Only remember, it's bound to get round the place that you've over 60,000 dollars' worth of pearls hidden aboard, as we're bound to believe; and if that tale goes round, look out for crooks! It'll be enough to bring all the man-eaters in the Bowery, trying to pay you a night visit. Well, so long, old man! The way of transgressors isn't exactly macadam, is it?"

You can imagine that what he had told me set me thinking after he had gone. I had never suspected the steward; for I had imagined that no one on the American side, either ashore or aboard, knew about the pearls, except the Customs and myself. Even then, I could not see how they could have heard anything definite; for the Customs officers are not in the habit of blabbing all round the place.

Suddenly, I slapped my knee. I remembered the first day in port, when I took Mac-Allister into my cabin, and both of us thought we heard some one at the door. That was Pelter, right enough. It couldn't very well be any one else, for both of my Mates were on deck at the time, and only the Steward could have entered the after cabin without being noticed.

I determined to lay a trap and began my preparations accordingly, the first of which was to secure a number of eggs from the pantry, some roping twine from a locker, a bottle of sepia and a camel-hair brush.

I made a tiny hole in each end of each egg, after which I blew them. When they were empty, I painted, with sepia, the brief legend "PEARLS" on each of the empty egg-shells. Then I strung the six of them together on the piece of roping-twine.

I went, then, into my cabin and shut the door; but instead of locking it I made fast one end of a piece of fine cotton to the hook-eye at the top of the door and led the free end over a long wire guide, which I arranged above my pillow.

To this end of the cotton I lashed my slightly wetted sponge, which was thus suspended directly above where my face would be when I was lying down. Whoever opened the door would, automatically, lower the wet sponge on to my face and so waken me without a sound.

Fortunately, we have the luxury of a dynamo, so that I could have the cabin lit up at any moment I wished by means of the bunk-switch, which was just to my hand, as I lay in my bunk. The "pearl" legended string of eggs I hung on to the knob of the switch.

After seeing that all was in working order, I took a revolver from my lock-up drawer and pushed it under my pillow as a handy adjunct in case of any unpleasantness. Then I turned in and went promptly to sleep. The wet sponge was my night watch.

I woke suddenly, with the chill of an impossible, cold wet thing upon my face. I reached up swiftly and caught the sponge—and remembered.

Without moving, I stared at the door and saw by the dim light from the saloon beyond that it was being slowly and gently closed. It shut without a sound, and there was an absolute darkness in my cabin, then the vague, soft sound of a bare foot upon the floor, and I knew that some one was in my cabin with me and was tiptoeing silently towards my bunk.

Very quietly, I reached up in the darkness to the switch with my left hand. I unhooked the string of empty egg-shells off the knob of the switch and transferred them to my right hand. Then I put up my left again to the switch and waited.

Suddenly I felt something touch me. A hand was feeling gently down my chest, towards my waist. It stopped there and began with infinite gentleness and an equally infinite patience to work at the buckles of my money-belt, which I find it advisable, in my wanderings among the "wits" of humanity, to wear next to my skin.

I waited a while, lying silent. There was evidently no thought of putting anything so uncomfortable as a knife between my ribs, so I thought it safe to pander somewhat to my curiosity. Possibly, whoever was in my cabin had the impression that I slept with sixty thousand dollars' worth of pearls round my waist! The thought tickled me.

For maybe a quarter of an hour I lay there, extremely awake and very curious to discover how the person in the dark would attempt to get the belt from under me after he had undone all the buckles. There are three of these to the belt, and I counted them, as the hidden personage worked them adrift.

As the last buckle was loosed, I was tickled to death, in more ways than one, to find how I was to be made roll over off the belt; for the infernal and silent personage in the dark reached down one hand to my feet and proceeded gently to tickle the sole of my left foot. I bit my lip to keep from laughing and found that he certainly knew his business; for I instinctively rolled away from him.

Doubtless, the plan is known by sneak-thieves to work perfectly on a sleeping person; but I was awake and found myself unable to hold back any longer.

I let out one enormous yell of laughter and in the same instant switched on the light and sat up, holding out the string of blown egg-shells to—Pelter, my Steward!

Yes, it was Pelter, right enough, and he shrivelled where he stood. He backed, quaking, his eyes staring at me, his face the color of chalk, and all his body arched half side-ways, in a very tension of the agony of complete and dreadful surprise. And there I sat in my bunk and roared, still holding out the string of egg-shells to him—those "pearls" that made no secret of the fact!

"Ah, Pelter," I said at last, still shaking, "they are yours, with my compliments. I have been expecting you to call." And I held the gorgeous necklace toward him, the while that his body arched more and more tensely toward the door, with the blind instinct of retreat.

Abruptly, his wit came back into him, and he turned and jumped for the door, tore it open, dashed through and slammed it.

    *   *   *   *

This morning I discovered that I am Pelterless!

    *   *   *   *

In a way, things are looking a bit serious. I've been searched every time I've gone ashore, and each time they've been pretty near as drastic as the first time. I fancy Monsieur, the Treasury Johnny, has his knife especially deep into me. Anyway, if I'd had the pearls on me I should have been caught, as sure as nuts are nuts.

I've done my best, up to the present, to keep my temper, but this kind of thing gets on one's nerves; and it's less the cash now that is keeping me fixed to run the pearls through, than the determination to put one over on the little comic Treasury man. I believe he's begun to dream of me at night. He's been in at the office several times lately and superintended the search himself, which I can see has annoyed MacAllister no end. I suppose the only thing is to keep on smiling!

Evening of July 5.

When I went ashore to-day, I took the six blown egg-shells with me, as I knew Mac would be interested, after his warning to keep an eye on Pelter.

"I've brought the six pearls," I said, as soon as I was ushered into the inner room, and I hauled out the string of egg-shells and held them up, so that Mac and the two officers could read the legend on each. Every one laughed, but they roared when I told them of the way I had treated the Steward. Yet, for all that they were so jolly and friendly, they searched me just as mercilessly as ever.

As I was going to leave the office, after my usual undress rehearsal, the little Treasury official came in.

I looked at MacAllister and winked; then turned towards the doorway.

"Good-morning, Sir," I said to the little man as he stood and glared at me. "You were a prophet. Your men have discovered six pearls of unsurpassable size upon me."

"What!" he shouted, and I heard the subordinate officials striving manfully with an inconvenient laughter.

"Where are the pearls, Mr. MacAllister?" called out the high official. "I knew we should catch the scoundrel if we searched him properly every time he went ashore. Let me see them. . . . You are under arrest!" (This last to me!) "Have you got all six, Mr. MacAllister? Let me see them at once."

"Here they are, Sir," I said. "Not exactly pearls of great price, but undoubtedly of wonderful size and shape!" And I drew out the six blown egg-shells and held them out, so that he might admire the fine black inscription on each.

"Allow me!" I said and stepped up to him. But as I made to wreath the "necklace" about his elderly neck, he lost control and made as if he would strike me.

"The gift is not acceptable?" I asked. "Gratitude is not in you, Sir! By-bye!"

And I left, just as MacAllister and the subordinate officials proved unable to rise to sufficiently heroic heights to die silently upon their feet. They crowed, all of them, like a farmyard, and then roared in hopeless unison. I could still hear them roaring as I boarded a street car to go up town.

As I was coming aboard again this evening I met MacAllister.

"You shouldn't do it, old man!" he said. "You shouldn't, and that's a sure thing! We laughed till we nearly fell down, and then old Andrew Akbotham fell on us. He's got a tongue that would make sulphur taste like cane sugar."

"Sorry," I said. "Where's he live? I'll write and smooth him down a bit."

He gave it me. This is the letter I wrote—

"Andrew Akbotham, Esq.,

   "DEAR SIR,

        "I feel that I owe you an apology for my hardly excusable buffoonery towards you. In evidence of my penitence, I beg you to accept as a little proof of my entire freedom from any thought of personal malice towards you the jewel box which accompanies this letter. The contents will interest you the more you examine them. You will find in the box the same six eggshells that I proffered you so uncouthly to-day. If you look at them closely you will see that they have been cut round the middle very neatly with a sharp razor and afterwards joined again with 'Mells' Lime Cement,' which, being made from ground egg-shells, makes a join that is quite invisible, except microscopically.

    "If you choose to break open one of the eggs, you will find inside, attached to the twine which runs through it, a small lump of cobbler's wax. In this, if you examine it, you will find an indentation, such as might be made by a marble, a large pill, or even a fine pearl.

"In each of the eggs you will find a similar pellet of cobbler's wax and a similar indentation—six in all.

"Need I say more, to prove to you the sincerity of my apologies and the truth of my explanations, when I say that nothing was further from my thoughts than practising mere gratuitous buffoonery upon a man of your years?

"May I beg of you to keep the jewel case and the six eggshells? They have done their work, twice over, as one might say. And I should like to feel that this apology of mine will be remembered long after I, its unworthy author, am forgotten.

   "Believe me, dear Sir,
    "Yours faithfully,
     "G. GAULT."

CHAPTER VII

Sailing ship *Alice Saunders,*
September 4.

"THIS shipping into a windjammer is a bit of a come-down for me, Sir," said my new Second Mate when I signed him on at the beginning of the voyage.

"Is it!" I said. "Well, Mister, there's men nearly as good as you made the change. I'm one of them; and let me tell you it has its compensations, as I'll show you, if you're the man I take you to be."

In a way, he was right! This is a bit of a come-down from passenger carrying, but it has its good points. There's less palaver, less starch and more rest—quite decidedly there's more rest! And, incidentally, more cash.

This may sound a bit funny, after my late forty a month, while now I'm getting only

183

fourteen-ten; but I was too much watched—
a deuced sight too much watched! In the
last three trips I was passenger-shunting I
never cleared more than an odd hundred,
over and above my pay.

September 9.

I've been too long out of sailing ships;
and I'm forgetting their little ways. I told
Mr. Parkins, the Second Mate, to keep the
sail on her, as I didn't want to be a year on
the passage. If he wanted to shorten down
he'd got to give me a call first. There's been
too much shortening down, to my mind! I
suppose I've got used to steam and a steady
number of knots per hour.

Anyway, Parkins carried on, to orders,
and now I've a sprung main-topmast.
That'll mean a fortnight's work when we
get into port and a new spare topmast.
Meanwhile, I've put a "bandage" round the
spar and am carrying less sail and a little less
cocksureness about things in general.

September 15. In Port (Havana).

I'm on to a problem that I hope may
prove good. The problem resolves itself

into something quite simple—to talk about!
That is, how to transfer two hundred thousand first-class cigars from this tight little
island bang into the warehouse of Messrs.
—— & Co., Liverpool. . . . No names mentioned! My share of the transaction to be
most of the work and all the risk (as usual)!
Incidentally I'm to have half the profits.
What they will be you can easily reckon out
if you will calculate the duty on two thousand boxes of a certain half-crown cigar you
no doubt often smoke, as I do always.

I make nothing on the freight; neither do
Messrs. —— nor Messrs. ——; for this sailing packet is the owners', and they run it
for profit, not for my pleasure; therefore
they shall receive full freightage, though I
shall pay it under the heading of personal
sundries, with weight and cubic details to
match!

September 18.

I've risked it and shipped a lot; but I'm
still in a bit of a haze, how I'm going to get
these sixteen hefty cases of contraband slap
into the warehouse of Messrs. —— & Co.,

right in the heart of Liverpool City. The details are more than I've been able to imagine, yet.

Meanwhile, I've got my other troubles, in the shape of rigging the new main-topmast. Chips has got it shaped out, and I've got a couple of new spares from ashore, and, generally, we're in a devil of a muddle.

October 13. At sea again.

I've been putting in a lot of thought how to get this contraband stuff through safely. It's no joke putting through sixteen big cases of cigars right under the noses of the Customs, as you can imagine; but I've got the major part of the plot all fixed, and, provided the Customs at Liverpool are not tipped off to make a special search, I've very good hopes of getting the stuff through; for the hiding-place I've got is cute enough to hide Charles the Second from a dozen hefty Cromwells.

October 28. Off Liverpool.

Did any one ever hear the like! I've just had a cypher wireless from the Agent ashore, to tell me that there's been a leakage. The Customs have got hold of the fact that I shipped two hundred thousand cigars in Havana, and they're just waiting to pounce on me as soon as they get aboard. Did any one ever hear such a thing! The fact that they know the exact quantity shows that they've got firsthand information from some sneak-eye somewhere the other end. And they'll be aboard inside of two hours!

The Agent insists that I must declare the stuff, and his firm will supply me privately with the cash to pay the duty. I can see he's in a proper funk! But if I pay the duty there'll not be a cent in the business for me.

Also, there's too much that's irregular about the whole business for me to expect to come off scot-free! If I'd not been out to smuggle the stuff, why did I ship it secretly, and then hide it—well, in the queer place where it is hidden and where it's not too easy to get at?

I guess it's easy to talk? I'm going to have a shot to run the stuff through yet. I must think; for there's got to be a mighty big alteration in all my little plans.

October 29. Liverpool.

I thought hard for a bit; then I went over to my "sender," for I have a two-hundred-mile radius installation, which I have fitted at my own expense. I sent a return cypher to the Agent, with one or two plain, healthy, vigorous words to help it along!

After that, I went up on deck and got hold of Mr. Allison, the First Mate.

I set out the situation to him and the Second Mate and made them both "interested" in the stuff getting safely ashore.

"Come along down with me and start to hide cigars for all you're worth!" I told the First Mate.

To the Second Mate I gave instructions to rig the cargo-gear, and to get gantlines up on the three masts, and start sending down the upper yards; for we're going up the Ship Canal, and the upper spars will have to come down, to go under the bridges.

"The busier we are at ship's work," I told him, "the more honest we'll look when the Custom sharks get aboard. So make things hum, Mister!"

Then the First Mate and I went below to

hide cigars. I hauled out boxes of cigars, and burst them open.

"Load as many up the inside of the stove flue as you can," I told the Mate. "It's an excellent place! I'll be unscrewing the top of the saloon table. There's a famous well underneath, the size of the whole table-top, and big enough to hold three layers of cigars at least. It should hold thousands, at a pinch."

Just then the Steward poked his head into the saloon.

"Get out of here, Steward, and keep out!" I told him. "Shut the door!"

"Can you trust him, Sir?" asked the Mate, from where he knelt, packing half-crown cigars up the flue, which, however, was as clean inside as salt water and elbow-grease could make it.

"Trust no one in this wicked world!" I told him. "I guess he's more to lose by chewing out any suspicions he's suffering from than by holding his tongue. The worst thing I know against him is, he's inclined to be sulky, and he's a deuce of a thief. He bought a box of rotten cigars in port, and he's smoked mine all the way home, and swears they're some of those he bought; but I can smell the difference the length of the decks. If the Customs happen to drop on any of the hidden cigars I'll swear I hid them from the Steward. It may sound a bit thin; but I'll declare a dozen boxes, just to cover the odd finds they're liable to make. Then they can't touch me, unless, of course, they find more than I've declared!"

I grinned at him.

"As for the Steward, whatever he suspects, he *knows* nothing that can do much harm. Not even you or the Second Mate knew about the stuff till I told you."

"That's the truth, Sir," said the Mate.

Jove! how we worked! I kept breaking open boxes of cigars, and as I emptied them I chucked the empty boxes out through the stern portholes into the river; for we were now in the estuary of the Mersey.

When, at last, I had loaded as many into the concealed "well," under the table-top, as I thought wise, I put the top back, and began to screw it down again.

"Get up on deck, Mister," I said to the

Mate, for we had put in a solid hour and a half's labor. "See if you can spot the Customs launch coming off. I'll finish here."

"Very good, Sir," he said, and put on his coat, and went on to the poop.

In less than ten seconds he came down the companion stairs with a jump.

"They're here, Sir!" he called out, quickly, shoving his head in through the saloon doorway. "They're alongside!"

"All right!" I said. "Don't get excited, for goodness' sake. I've got to bluff them. I'll swear they've got hold of a mare's nest. Now get up on to the poop and stand around handy. Tell the officer in charge that I'm down here."

"Very good, Sir," said my First Mate, and raced up again on to the poop.

A minute later, I heard the tramp of feet on the poop deck above me, and I slung the screwdriver I had been using under the table.

"Good-morning, Captain Gault," said the head officer of the Customs, as he came into the saloon. He was a man I didn't know; for I've not been into this port of late.

"Morning," I said. "Will you come into my cabin, Mister?"

As I spoke, I saw that he was shooting glances all round the place. And then, suddenly, as if to catch me unexpectedly, he whipped round on me with a sharp—

"Anything to declare, Cap'n Gault?"

He began to reel off the usual list, but I checked him.

"It's all right!" I said. "I know it all by heart. I've got twelve boxes of a hundred cigars each to declare, and nothing more of any kind."

I said it with a bit of a snap; for the beggar had something about him that put my back up.

He turned to the two men who had followed him down, and nodded; then he came round on me again.

"You stick to that, Captain Gault, do you?" he asked.

"Certainly," I said. "What is more, allow me to explain that I dislike your manners, your method of pronouncing your words, and your breath. The last is particularly displeasing. You should smoke better cigars!"

The man stared at me as if he thought I was mad; but before he could get out any expressions of easement I concluded—

"Perhaps, Mister," I said, "you'll finish your examination of the cabins as quick as you can, and get out of here. You're in my way. I've declared twelve hundred cigars, and they're for my own smoking" (which last fact was strictly true). "Now get on with your searching, or you'll not be done to-day. You've all the rest of the ship to attend to yet!"

"Damn your impudence!" he sung out. "I never heard the like of you before. I declare, you're——" But what other qualities of mine he was going to praise I can't say, for at that moment one of his two men caught his arm, and as he turned I heard the man say, quite distinctly, in an excited whisper—

"They're down here, Sir. Jock's just had a word with the Steward."

The Customs officer came round on me again.

"Now, my man," he began; but I pulled him up sharp.

"Say 'Sir,' I told him, or 'Captain Gault'!"

He went quite white at that in his attempt to hold back the temper I had risen in him.

"I'll make you eat humble-pie in half a moment!" he said, in a quiet voice that was, yet, actually husky with the temper I'd prodded into healthy activity. "Now, quit your damned fooling. You've declared twelve hundred cigars, but *we* happen to know you've two hundred thousand aboard. They're down here, and we're going to find them. You may as well own up!"

"You're on to a mare's nest!" I told him. "I've got just twelve one-hundred boxes of cigars."

"Where are they?" he slapped back at me. "Out with them!"

"All right!" I said; and then I saw the Steward looking in, over the shoulders of the two men.

"Get out of here, Steward!" I said. "And you others, too, while I get out my cigars. I'll not have any one know where I choose to hide my stuff. Take the Steward out with you, and shut the door. I'll call out when you're to come in. I'll not have the Steward see where they are. He's a thief——"

"You're a liar!" shouted the Steward, at the top of his voice. "A damned liar!"

And at that I went for him; but the officer and his two men got hold of me, and for a moment I nearly lost my temper!

I took no more direct notice of the Steward; but spoke again to the officer.

"Let go of my jacket! Confound your infernal insolence!" I said. "I've twelve hundred cigars to declare, do you hear me? Twelve hundred cigars! Got that into your thick head? Twelve hundred cigars!" I shouted it in their faces, at the top of my voice. "Here! If you don't believe me, get out of here! . . . On deck there! On deck there!" I yelled. "On deck there!"

There was a sudden running of feet, and the Mate came crashing and clattering down the stairs into the saloon. He carried a heavy capstan-bar in his fists.

One of the Customs men loosed me and jumped at him. He caught him round the body, and started to wrestle with him lustily, with all his might; while the officer lugged out a big silver whistle, on the end of a chain, and whistled, till the saloon rang and piped again with the shrill sound.

There was a rush of feet along the poop deck, and several Customs officials came racing down the companion-way stairs into the saloon.

"Arrest these two for obstruction!" yelled the head officer.

"Obstruction be jiggered!" I shouted. "Obstruction be jiggered! I'm obstructing nobody. Do you hear me? I'm obstructing nobody. I've stated that I've twelve hundred cigars to declare, and I've declared them till I've got a sore throat. Do you hear me? I've declared twelve hundred—— Here! let go of me!"

"Hold him!" shouted the head officer.

"Hold them both! Peters, down with that funnel——"

"If you'll get out of here, and take the Steward with you," I called out, "I'll get you the cigars myself, without your breaking or unshipping anything. But I'll not let the Steward see where I keep my stuff.

I've missed over fifty on the trip home——"

"You're a liar, Sir!" shouted the Steward's voice, fiercely, from the doorway.

"Hold your tongue!" sung out the Mate. "If I put my hands on you, I'll learn you manners to the Cap'n!"

"Silence!" shouted the head officer. Then, as the Mate began to fight his way towards the Steward, there was quite a dust-up in the saloon, until about four of them went down in a heap on him.

"Get at that table, Jackson," said the head officer. "It's screwed."

"Suppose some of you get off the Mate's head!" I called out. "There's plenty of chairs in the place. You might let him breathe, now and then, for a change!"

"Si—lence!" shouted the officer. Then to the men: "Let him up, but keep hold of him."

As the First Mate got to his feet, and saw that they had started to unscrew the top of the saloon table, he swore!

"Yes!" said the head officer, grimly. "We've got you where we want you, this time. We've been tipped off that you've

tried a big speculation, but it's impossible to
do that kind of thing now-a-days; as you
should know, if you'd the sense of sheep.

. . . Billy, hand me out those boxes
we picked up. I told you to shove 'em in
the Steward's pantry, handy for when we
wanted them."

The man Billy loosed the Mate, and
stepped out into the pantry. He came back
in a few moments, with a great stack of
empty cigar-boxes, that still dripped salt
water. I recognized them, and stared at
the Mate. He stared back at me, silent.

"You see, you're done, finished—knocked
out!" said the head officer. "You'll do
time for this bit of business. You'll——"

"It's a lie!" sung out the First Mate.
"It's some lie that Steward's been stuffing
you with."

"That's it," I said. "A thief's bound to
be a liar."

"Liar yourself, Cap'n!" sung out the
Steward, obviously insolent because he knew
he was safe. "You got thousands and mil-
lions of ceegars; and maybe I'd not have
split, only you was that stingy. I don't

mind a bit of smuggling, not on principle; but I expects to have *my* share, and if I don't get it, I guess I does the other thing. . . . It's your own fault, Cap'n. I'd have stuck by you if you'd have give me my share. I would——"

"What's all that?" called out the officer. "You be careful what you're saying, my lad, or you'll be in chokee along with the Captain and the Mate."

He turned to his own men.

"That'll do, Billy and Saunders," he said. "You two can go up on deck, and finish there; we'll be able to manage these two now, I guess."

Saunders was one of the men who were holding me; and as soon as he let go, I made one dive for the Steward, who was playing Tunes of Insolence, in which his nose and right thumb made a displeasing conjunction.

"Let's lamn the animal, Sir!" I heard the Mate shout, as I made my charge; and I knew that the two of us were truly bent to a single purpose.

"Hold them!" I heard the officer shout.

"Hold them!" And then his men were hanging on to me like a lot of rats, and there was quite some energy adrift in the saloon.

During the hullabaloo, the man who was working at the table-top continued stolidly to unscrew screws; and presently, when the Mate and I decided on a mutual rest, the man sung out to some one to come and give him a lift.

As the table-top came off, there was a mutter of exclamation from the Customs men, to see the cigars lying there in a brown layer. Immediately afterwards, the man with the screwdriver, who had pushed his fingers down into the shallow well, called out that there weren't above eight or nine hundred.

"I told you that I declared only twelve boxes of a hundred each!" I said. "Did you suppose they were going to have young ones? The others are up the flue. And you'll not find another, if you hang on to my jacket till you turn gray!"

Neither did they find one, though they turned the saloon and the cabins upside down, and finally the lazarette underneath.

Eventually, the Second Mate came down into the saloon, to ask whether he was supposed to be in sole charge of the ship, or what. And, at that, the head officer had to give orders to his men to release us. A precious fool he must have felt; and, as I explained to him, I was not at all sure that I had not got a case against him for assault and false imprisonment! For he had certainly made prisoners of the Mate and me in my own saloon.

However, I told him that I was inclined to mercy; and that, no doubt, when he was older, he would look back with gratitude to the old sea-captain who was too soft-hearted to ruin the career of a young, though insolent, Customs officer, merely to gratify a feeling of indignation, however righteous! Finally, I insisted on shaking hands with him, which he submitted to in a stupified sort of way.

"What's your name, Mister?" I asked him.

"Grey," he answered, still in a dazed kind of fashion. You see, he'd been so certain sure of finding the stuff down aft; and, I daresay, my friendly way rather staggered him!

"Well, Mr. Grey," I said, "away and do your duty. There's all the rest of the ship to search yet; and as you say I've two hundred thousand cigars aboard, you shouldn't have much trouble in locating them!

"When you come to think of it, two hundred thousand cigars would take up a lot of room; why, they'd pretty well fill a whole cabin from deck to deck—eh? Now, don't you see, Mister, the whole foolishness of what you've been told? No Ship-Master, in his senses, would try to run a cabinful of cigars through the Customs. It couldn't be done. Some joker's been pulling your leg! But if you still think I'm clever enough to magic wholesale orders of that kind past you, why, just turn-to on the ship again; and afterwards, when you've found nothing (for I'm betting that's all you will find!), come along aft, and own up you've been fooled!"

But my little talk never stopped him one

bit. He seemed to get a fresh notion, and went racing up on deck to test it, and I went after him, to see what it was.

As you know, I'd given the Second Mate orders to start sending down the upper yards, so as to be ready for our trip up the Ship Canal. Well, what did your Mister Customs Officer do but have the plugs taken out of all the hollow steel yards that had been lowered, to make sure that I'd not packed them with cigars.

Of course, there was nothing in them; but that didn't satisfy him. He sent his man aloft, and they took out the cross-bolts and worked out the plugs from the ends of every yard aloft. And when they found nothing there, they examined the hollow steel topmasts and lower masts. Then they came down to the hull again, and tried the spare wooden topmast and royal masts, that were lashed along under the bulwarks. But they were just plain, sound, natural wood.

They were still at it last evening, when we tied up in Ellesmere Port, in the Canal. I could see that the Customs must have had pretty certain information, to waste time like that.

Last night they kept a watch of two men aboard; and to-day they've had more men down, to tackle the three holds, and they're simply *proving* to themselves that the cigars are not aboard.

November 3, Evening.

The Customs have at last assured themselves that I'm neither as illegal as a magician nor as big a liar as the man who cabled them misleading cigar-shaped news from Havana.

They gave up the search last night, after three agitated days of it. During these three days I've got quite friendly with the head officer; and when he gave me a clean sheet, and called his men off to something more useful, I invited myself ashore with him, for I was going into Liverpool for the evening.

"Look here," I said, as we climbed out at Liverpool, "you're off duty now, aren't you?"

"Yes," he replied. "My time's my own now, till to-morrow—— Why?"

"Well," I told him, "if you're off duty,
I guess we can bury the hatchet. So come
and have a quiet dinner with me, and I'll
tell you a bit of a yarn, as between man and
man."

He came, and this is the yarn I told him,
over the wine—

"A friend of mine, just a plain, ordinary
seafaring man, shipped two hundred thousand cigars aboard, on the strict Q.T. When
he reached England, he got word that
the Customs had received 'certain information'; the said information being horribly
correct.

"My friend thought for a while; then he
acted. He broke open a number of cigar-
boxes, and hid all his personal smokes in the
saloon. He pitched the boxes out through
the after port-holes, for he knew that sharp
eyes were sure to be watching his ship; but
he left nothing to chance. He had a quiet
word or two with his Steward.

" 'Steward,' he said, 'when the Custom
House officers come aboard, you can let them
know, in a friendly sort of way, that there
are possibly some cigars hidden in the sa-

loon. Also, if I should chance to tell you to your face just what a damned thief you are, you need not bother to be as polite as courage might suggest. Got that?'

" 'Yes, Sir,' said the Steward. 'I s'pose there'll be. something in it for me if I does it all right and proper?'

" 'Five quid, my lad,' he told him.

" 'I'll earn 'em, Sir,' said the Steward, fervently.

"And so, it happened that when the Customs officers boarded my friend's ship, they had not only the information which the floating cigar-boxes had given them of cigars hastily hidden, but they were aided in their search by timely suggestions from the Steward.

"My friend was careful to declare the exact number of cigars that the officers would be likely to find, and offered to produce them, if they would vacate the saloon for a while; which, of course, he knew they would not do.

"He then shouted for his First Mate, who had been carefully primed. The First Mate came racing down into the saloon, without waiting even to drop the capstan-bar which he had in his hands. This studied omission imparted a warlike effect to him; yet there was no intention of (or need for) violence; but the head officer of the Customs searchers saw intentions to offer fight, and he whistled for all his men to come to the rescue.

"They did so, and my friend and his First Mate were somewhat roughly handled. They received further rough treatment when they evinced an unnatural desire to chastise the insolence of the Steward.

"But, finally, when no cigars were discovered, over and above those which had been declared, the Custom House officer had to order the release of my friend and his First Mate.

"For three days the Customs infested the vessel; and at last had to admit that there was no such thing as a secret consignment of cigars aboard, and that they had been misled, through acting upon 'uncertain' information!

"And yet the two hundred thousand cigars *were* aboard.

"You will remember that my friend acted

peculiarly in the cabin, hiding no more cigars than he intended to declare. Also, his calling for the First Mate was curious, and their united and earnest desire to hammer the Steward was also somewhat, shall I say, abnormal.

"You will be able to understand the plot better when I tell you that, at the very moment when my friend and his First Mate and Steward were 'entertaining' the whole of the Customs officials in the saloon, the two hundred thousand cigars were being hoisted over the side, under the superintendence of the Second Mate, into a launch, which my friend had arranged to run alongside on a given signal from the deck.

"You will see now that *all* that went on in the saloon was nothing more than a lure and a ruse, intended to get all the Customs men aboard below, and keep them interested there, whilst the two hundred thousand cigars were being transhipped to the launch.

"You might ask, however, how it was that none of the watchful eyes ashore noticed this somewhat unusual act of unloading. And would not the engineer who was left in the Customs launch think there was something wrong?

"The explanation is simple. My friend was safe from suspicion, either from those ashore, or from the Customs engineer, through the following causes: First, because the official watchers ashore would not sussuspect a vessel which had the Customs launch alongside, and the officers actually aboard. Second, the engineer never saw the other launch, because it came up on the opposite side of the vessel. Third, because no cases were lowered over the side; for the two hundred thousand cigars were all hidden, in sixteen tin cases, inside a dummy 'spare' topmast, in which they were actually shipped aboard out abroad. And as the Second Mate was lowering spars from aloft, there was nothing particularly noteworthy in the fact that one of the spars at the end of his tackle happened to be that genuine-looking, but exceedingly valuable, spare topmast.

"And, of course, as soon as it was in the water, the launch took it in tow, and went off, away and away-oh!

"Neat of my friend, wasn't it?" I asked.

"You cunning devil!" said the Customs Officer.

CHAPTER VIII

CONTRABAND OF WAR

s.s. *John L. Sullivan,*
May 15.

ONE of the main-hatch slings bust again this morning, and lost a lot of heavy crated goods over the side.

This is the second time a sling has parted in the last couple of days.

"Mr. Anwyn," I said to the First Mate, "scrap every one of those confounded cargo slings at once. You ought never to have lifted another ton with them, after that one parted yesterday. I'll not have another thing hoisted out of the holds until you've new slings. Use some of that new coil of four-inch manilla; and get some of the men on the job, smart. We're just wasting money, keeping the lighters idle. You ought not to have needed me to tell you a thing like this!"

I let the Mate see what I felt in the matter, and I said what I had to say flat out before Mr. Jelloyne, the tally clerk; for there was no excuse for the thing happening twice, and I had a right to feel warm.

This unloading into lighters is a slow, weary job at best, and it will take us another week or ten days to clear the cargo out of her.

May 16.

Mr. Jelloyne, the tally clerk, is certainly a bit of a character. He was talking this morning about the government restrictions on landing war material, and the difficulty of doing it secretly.

The old chap seems quite what one might call a bit of a sport.

"Would you do it, Mr. Jelloyne, if you got a chance?" I asked him; for I was more than simply curious to find out how he looked at a thing of that kind.

He took a glance round, and then came closer to me.

"It all depends, Cap'n," he said. "There's a lot of cash in it; but getting caught is a serious business."

"But if you were practically *sure* of not being caught?" I suggested.

"Ah!" he said, and winked at me. "Who wouldn't undertake it, under those conditions!"

That was enough for one time, and I said nothing more to him, until this afternoon, when we got talking about it again. He was contending that, apart from the disagreeables attendant upon capture, the thing was enormously difficult. He instanced some of the difficulties.

First, an "examination" of the ship's manifest, showing what she was carrying.

Second, the booking down (or "tallying") of every case and article hoisted out of the hold of every ship in the bay, by the clerk sent aboard each ship.

Third, the examination of every lighter-load sent ashore. If any cases went astray between the ship and the shore, a comparison of the tally clerk's tally-book, with the Customs officials' checking of the load would show instantly that a case or article was missing.

Fourth, any suspicious-looking case might

be opened by the Authorities, to verify that its contents were as per ship's manifest.

Fifth, if any vessel tried to unload cargo secretly after dark, she was bound to be discovered, because her hatches were sealed every night by the Government official on the last tug, and were broken by him each morning when he came round on the first tug.

Sixth, there was a night patrol boat, which kept an eye on things in general, and especially on any vessel that acted in any way out of the ordinary, or which did any noticeable amount of boat-traffic with the shore, or even with other vessels lying out in the bay.

"Makes it quite a pleasantly interesting mental problem to see how it might be managed," I said. "I don't think it would be very difficult. . . . One might make the tally clerk a present of a hundred quid, on a big job, not to 'tally' down a case of contraband now and again."

Old Mr. Jelloyne shook his head at that.

"No good, Captain!" he said. "No man is going to risk losing his billet for that kind of thing. Why, he'd be at the mercy of any one who felt like talking."

"Not my notion of a clever job," I told him. "If I were the kind of man who would do things of that sort, Mr. Jelloyne, I'd try to make it interesting to carry out. For instance, one could avoid the sealing of the hatches, by cutting through into the hold from the lazarette under the main cabin. The stuff could be brought up through the cabin without ever touching the sealed hatches. That is one of the big difficulties overcome."

"What about these same cases being missing when we come to compare the tally-book with the ship's manifest?" he asked me.

"That's certainly a difficulty," I admitted; "but it would simply have to be ignored. By the time the cases were proved missing, they'd be away and away-oh, ashore."

"Then, again, I'd avoid the port risks, and minimize the chance of the patrol-boat dropping on me, by moving the ship over nearer to the North shore. There are plenty of lonely bits of quiet beach there, where I could make a quick dash with a boat-load, now and again at night, if I watched when the patrol-boat was over on the other side of the bay."

Mr. Jelloyne grinned at me in his wicked old way.

"It *might* do," he admitted. "It's plain and simple. Perhaps it's just as well you're not in the business, Captain!"

"My goodness!" I wanted to shout, "I've two thousand pounds' worth of rifles to smuggle ashore, if you only knew it!"

But I took jolly good care not to, as you may think.

"As you remarked just now, Mr. Jelloyne," I said, passing him my case, "it's a mighty risky business. And a sea-captain's like the Law: he should be above suspicion."

"Quite right, Captain. Quite right, Captain," he said, heartily; and I let it drop at that.

May 17.

We've been riding to one anchor since we've been here; but last night there was a strong breeze from the southeast that made us drag for nearly a mile. I let her drag; for there's plenty of room, and it suited my purpose. Then I let go the second bower, and that brought her up.

"You've dragged, Cap'n, during the night," said old Mr. Jelloyne, when he came out this morning. "That was a stiff little blow you had out here. I never thought the sea would have been quiet enough for the lighters this morning, and I'd promised myself a day off. But there's no rest for the wicked."

"Yes," I told him, "it was quite a smart little breeze. I'm going to shift over to the north side. It's nearer in; but the holding's better."

When the tug came out with the second string of lighters, I arranged with the Captain to go ahead of us, while we hove up, and then to give us a tow across to the north side, where, as I told Mr. Jelloyne, the holding is admitted to be better. . . . All the same, I had my own notion that we had dragged simply because we must have fouled our anchor; but I did not elaborate the idea. I have waited a couple of weeks for just such a breeze, and I have been fully aware that our anchor must have been fouled for some days.

By such means as these, I have been able to bring my ship over nearer to the north shore, without exciting any unnecessary comment.

Night.

What old Mr. Jelloyne, the tally clerk, told me about the patrol-boat is quite correct. She was lying near us for some time to-night, out in the darkness, about four or five hundred yards away; I spotted her through my night-glasses. Evidently, the officer in charge wants to make sure there's nothing behind my moving the ship over here. Of course, I've simply watched the boat, and said nothing, except had a quiet sniggle to myself.

May 22.

To-night is to be the night. I've given the patrol-boat time to get used to my ship being here.

They had the patrol-boat near the ship most of the night of the 17th and again on the 18th; but I guessed they'd tire of that!

I just looked upon it as a mild diversion, watching them through my night-glasses. They must have been fools not to realize that a good pair of glasses must show them up plain on the water!

However, the last three nights they appear to have got settled in their minds that there's no especial need to keep their eyes glued on my ship all night long. And so to-night, the Firm ashore being now ready to remove the goods, I'm going to attempt to complete my little investment in rifles. If all goes well, I stand to clear a thousand pounds to my own cheek, and the money is as acceptable as money always is to a man of my somewhat developed tastes. I've rather stretched my finances lately, buying a Guido, which I could not let pass me.

I went ashore this morning, and got into final touch with the consignees. I took elaborate precautions to insure a secrecy as perfect as ever my heart could desire, and I know that there can have been no dangerous information leaking into the wrong quarters.

The arrangements are, that if I decide,

last thing, to send the stuff ashore, I am to have the House-Flag checked when lowering it at sunset, and re-hoisted, as if the signal haul-yards had fouled and needed clearing. Then the flag can be lowered in the usual way.

This is to be taken to mean that I will bring the boat ashore, with certain cases, any time after eleven o'clock, the exact time being impossible to fix, owing to the chance of the patrol-boat being on my side of the bay at the time.

Just before I leave the ship I am to flash a bull's-eye over the rail—the signal to be two long flashes and two short.

As an additional precaution for the success of my little adventure, I have had the boat I shall use painted a dead-colored gray, which should make it almost invisible at night; and new leathers on all the oars, to make them quieter in the rowlocks. The rendezvous is a little bit of lonely beach right opposite the ship.

May 23.

From sunset until eleven o'clock I kept an eye for the patrol-boat. She came over to our side the bay about 10.45 but did not stay more than a few minutes; and as soon as she had gone well away towards the south side I gave word to haul up the boat, which was lying astern, and to hoist into her, four big cases, that have been snugly out of sight down in the lazarette.

It was a very dark, quiet night, and just before giving the flashes with the bull's-eye, I thought I heard somewhere, far away over the water, and vague, the low, dull beat of a petrol-launch.

I told the men to come up out of the boat, and have a smoke for half an hour. Then I went up on to the bridge with my night-glasses, and had a good look to the south-east; but, so far as I could see, there was no sign of anything moving out in the bay. Then I examined the water between my ship and the shore; but this was quite clear of any craft.

I put in a full half hour, listening and watching the bay; but there was not a single thing to make me uneasy, and at last I sent word for the men to lay aft again into the boat.

I gave the required lamp-flashes; then I went down into the boat, and we pulled out from the ship's side. I headed her for the shore, steering for the dip in the cliffs that marked the beach.

"Gently, men, gently! No hurry!" I told them.

All the time, as we moved quietly shore-wards, I kept my eyes about me and my ears open; but there was not a thing of any kind to bother me, that I could see or hear; yet all the time I had a vague excitement of expectancy on me, that kept me a little tense, as may be supposed.

"Easy there. In bow!" I gave the word, as we drew in under the shadow of the cliffs. "Get up in the bows with the boathook, Svenson, and stand by to fend her off."

Though I spoke quietly, the words echoed back in a soft, curious echo from the low cliffs.

"That sounded funny, Sir," said the Third Mate, who was sitting by me.

"Only the echo," I told him; and as I spoke, the boat grounded on the soft sand of the beach, and the men were tumbling out on the instant, pell-mell, to haul her up.

"Out with the stuff, men," I said, as I jumped ashore.

As the last of the four big cases was landed on the sand, the Third Mate touched my arm.

"Hark, sir," he said, quickly. "What was that? . . . Look, Sir, what's that up the beach?"

I bent forward, and stared. As I did so, there was a sharp command out of the darkness up the beach.

"Hands up, or we fire!" shouted the voice.

"Copped, by the Lord!" said the Third Mate, and whirled round instinctively to the boat.

"Stop that, Mister!" I said. "Do you want to get us all filled with lead? The Authorities in this part shoot first and inquire afterwards! Put your hands up, men, all of you. And leave the talking to me."

As I spoke, I heard the pom, pom, pom, of petrol engines, and knew it was the sound of the patrol-boat coming full-tilt across the bay to cut off our retreat.

Then there came from up the beach the

flash of several police-lanterns; and as the
beams of light circled and rested on us, I
could see what a confoundedly absurd spec-
tacle we all looked, every man with his
hands reached up so earnestly to the black
heavens!

"Well," I said, staring, and trying to see
the men behind the lanterns, "what the
devil's this mean? Are you a hold-up, or
what?"

Of course, I knew it was bound to be the
Authorities, right enough; but I wanted
badly to blow off at them, or somebody. It
was plain there had been a leakage somewhere.

"Well," I said again, "what is it? What
the deuce is it? I can't stand here all
night!"   .

Then, out of the darkness behind the
bull's-eye lantern, stepped the Port Officer,
and informed me that I and my men were
under arrest for attempting to run a cargo of
rifles into the country.

"Don't talk rot," I told him. "Keep your
hands still, men," I said. "Leave this to
me. . . . Don't you think, Officer, you

and I could fix this up, without importing
my men or your men into it?   Let us take
a quiet walk up the shore, while I put a
proposition to you."

There was a roar of laughter from his own
men in the darkness behind the lanterns.
But the Port Officer did not laugh.

"Quit your fooling, Captain," he said.
"You may find yourself in extra trouble
over this job, for attempting bribery, if you
don't keep the lid on a bit more.   Don't you
get imagining you can bribe me or my men.
We're not bribable."

"Go and boil your head," I advised, as
mildly as the sentiment implied admitted.
"You annoy me incredibly. You're troubled
with a badly enlarged liver."

"See you," he said, stepping up close to
me, "if you don't drop that sort of talk,
you're going to get a hammering, right here
and now."

"Not by a puffy child like you," I said;
for it was part of my intention to aggravate
him to the limit.   And I did this sooner
than I expected; for, without a word further, he hit me with the back of his hand

across the mouth, while I stood helpless, with my hands above my head. I am, perhaps rather narrow-mindedly, glad to assert that he was not a countryman of mine. At the time it would not have mattered if he had been.

I just dropped my hands, and hit him as hard and solid as I could, right and left— one flat in the middle of his bread-machinery, and the other equally in the middle of his face—not scientific blows, perhaps; but they were so hearty and soundly-intentioned that he went nearly a dozen paces, spinning on his feet before he fell.

My men shouted and dropped their hands, and I leaned quickly towards the Third Mate.

"There's going to be a rumpus," I whispered. "While it's on, collar one or two of the men, and shove those cases down into the sea. Quick, now! I don't fancy there'll be any shooting."

I was completely right; for, if the Port Officer was no sportsman, his men were splendidly so. Down went their rifles with a crash, and they leaped to meet my men.

I fancy there must have been a good many Irishmen among them, from the intoning of their joyous and entirely improper and separate litanies. My men were mostly Scots, and they did very well in the fighting line (as later comparisons showed); but they were less fluent, or perhaps, to be strictly accurate, quite as persistent; but eventually a trifle monotonous!

How the fight went for a bit I could not tell; for every lantern had been put out in the first rush; moreover, I was dealing with the Port Officer in a way that I felt should prove memorable. I'll admit that he made lusty objections; but I'm nearer fifteen than fourteen stones, and I never did run to fat.

* * * *

When at last the lanterns were lit again, I found my men all handcuffed in a row, and looking as if they had thoroughly enjoyed themselves.

There were twenty of the Government men—big, hefty lads they were, too, and not one of them but had to choke a grin when I assisted the Port Officer politely to his feet.

"Now, Sir," I said, "perhaps you will

kindly explain the whole of this business, and the meaning of your unwarrantable and illegal assault upon my person."

The idiot glared at me; but had not a word to say. In any case, a violent loss of teeth does not improve articulation.

"The cases!" he shouted to his men, in a thick voice.

"They're gone clean away, Sir," said one of his men, after a brief search.

He grew frantic.

"Don't you tell me *that* for a yarn, you blind dummies," he shouted. "Look about! Look about! They're bound to be near."

I smiled; for the Third Mate had done very well indeed. Meanwhile, he and his men searched everywhere, more and more bewildered; until at last one of them spotted the corner of one of the cases sticking up above the water, where the Third Mate and one of the men had sunk them, during the row.

It took the Officer and his men half an hour to salvage the cases, and every man was wet through by the time they were hauled ashore.

As the big cases were taken from the sea, the water rushed out of holes that had been bored in them; and one of the men remarked this to the Port Officer, who snatched a lamp and began to examine the cases.

"Knock in the top of one of them!" he said, suddenly.

One of his men brought an axe from up the beach, and in a minute he had the side of one of the boxes laid right open.

"Empty!" shouted every one of his men, and my Third Mate as well; but the Port Officer said not a word. He seemed stunned for the moment.

"The—the others!" he said, at last. "Quick!"

But the other boxes were empty also, as they could tell by lifting them, now that the sea-water had drained out.

"Perhaps now, Sir, you will take that same little stroll along the beach, which I requested a while ago," I said. "If you had courteously acceded to my request, all this melodrama might have been omitted."

He stared at me, a moment, in a kind of dazed sulkiness.

"Meanwhile," I added, "you may as well give orders for my men to be released. I don't fancy it will pay you to keep them longer in that condition; for, as things are, you stand the chances of getting into serious trouble for your action to-night, in assaulting and arresting a body of law-abiding men, who have come ashore for no other object at all than to have a quiet little evening's 'gam' on the beach, with a bit of a bonfire made out of these old cases we've brought ashore, and towards which you seem to have exhibited extraordinary covetousness." ·

"Oh, stow it!" he muttered, wearily. "I'll come with you and hear what you've got to say."

He beckoned to his sub.

"Unlock them!" he ordered, and turned and followed me twenty or thirty yards up the beach.

"Now," he said, "be quick with what you wanted to tell me!" ·

"You've already learned, by ocular proof, as I might say, the major portion of it," I told him. "There are, however, one or two details to add. In the first place, I hap-

pened to receive information from a friend
that old Mr. Jelloyne was 'one of'yours,' so
I outlined to him just such a little outing as
to-night's, only with rifles in those cases, instead of air.

"He courteously performed his share of
my little plot by detailing my talk to you!
I then shifted my ship over to this side, and
when all was ready I went ashore and gave
information, per telephone, to your office,
that the s.s. *John L. Sullivan* would make
certain signals this evening to inform certain confederates ashore that her captain
would land a consignment of contraband of
war secretly to-night.

"I explained exactly what these signals
would be; and when you grew too grate-
fully insistent for the name of the 'man on
the 'phone,' I told you it was someone who
would see you personally, at the right moment, and define his reward. This is, if you
will allow me to say so, the right moment.

"There are just one or two minor details
unexplained. My men were not in this plot
at all. The Third, however, was fooled in
exactly the same way that you were; for I

told him secretly that there was contraband in the cases. He must have thought it mighty light contraband!

"By the way, don't you think the painting of the boat was a splendid little touch on my part to lend actuality to my, shall I call it, practical joke?

"In many ways, this joke is almost the best part of to-night's work. You see, it was so essential to draw all official attention away from our old berth in the bay; for some days ago, Mr. Officer, we broke (not quite by accident) a couple of slings, and there fell over the ship's side four cases of rifles, labeled sewing machines.

"These cases had been previously roped together, in couples, to facilitate a grapple finding them, and were picked up to-night (as a lantern signal informed me some fifteen minutes ago) by friends of mine ashore, while you and the patrol-launch have been attending my little burlesque here.

"Don't you think, now, it was all distinctly neat? And I stand to clear quite a thousand on the job.

"Shall we go back now? You see, dear

man, there have been no witnesses to this little talk; so you can prove nothing, and certainly nothing to *your credit,* while I can prove a great deal that is not to yours. Shall we call the game even?

"By the way, I can confidently recommend a raw beef-steak for black eyes. . . ."

CHAPTER IX.

THE GERMAN SPY

s.s. *Galatea,*
July 22.

"THERE'S one thing about taking charge of a tramp steamer;" I said yesterday to Mr. MacWhirr, the chief engineer, "one does get some variety; and if the pay is rather watery, there are little ways of making ends meet!"

This was when I was explaining what I wanted him to do.

I am drawing just seventeen-ten a month in this boiler, and that's a rise on the last Skipper, who was getting only fourteen-ten; but I struck at that!

I told Mr. Johnson, our owner, it wouldn't pay my washing, tobacco and wine bills. He laughed at the "joke," as he thought it; but there's more truth in it than he could ever understand.

The little commissioned piece of work I was talking over with MacWhirr comes off to-night. I am just jotting this down, while I have a quiet smoke, before getting busy.

We shall be off Toulon at 10.30. La Seyne comes after that, and I reckon to be off Sanary before 11.30. That's the place where I've got the £500 commission. There's a German ashore there, one of these spies, I suppose; and he's got plans that I'm to buy from him for the tidy sum of £2,000, in English bank-notes. How they do love English money! And how I do hate the spy brand, that haven't even the decency to spy for their own Fatherland; but do the dirty work of any confounded country that'll pay them a good figure.

I've my own idea what the plans are, and I shall have a good look at them, too.

I'm to get the German aboard and land him safe in Spain. I'm to meet him (his name is Herr Fromach) on the Point Issol at 12.30, exactly. If he is not there I am to wait half an hour. If he has not turned up then, I am free to come away, as it may be presumed (from what I can understand) that Herr Fromach will by then have been captured, and will be probably inspecting the inside of some kind of a French lock-up. I expect he'll get a private leathering, too, from the men who catch him; for I understand it is generally known ashore that the plans have been stolen by this same Herr; and feeling is running high among the Frenchmen; and there are search parties loose on all the mountains round Sanary; for they've got word he's hiding somewhere about there.

If I don't get him to-night, he'll almost certainly be caught; but I've given my word to do my best; and £500 isn't to be sniffed at!

There will be some risk attached, as people don't offer five-hundred-pound commissions merely for the trouble of embarking a casual passenger aboard a cargo tramp!

*   *   *   *

I had a wireless to-night from a "mutual friend" ashore. (I have fitted up a two hundred-mile radius installation aboard here at my own expense.) He warned me, as a friend, that the search is getting so hot and close I had better drop the whole busi-

ness, and not come ashore at all; for there
has been a leakage somewhere, and the authorities know that Herr Fromach is to attempt an escape from Sanary Bay to-night.

All this was, of course, in cypher, and I
replied, in cypher, that I had promised to be
on the Point Issol, near the Old Mill, from
12.30 midnight to one o'clock, and that
nothing short of a gun-boat would stop me
from being there. I nearly told him that
seventeen-ten a month was badly needing
supplementing, or else I should have to go
unlaundried; but I thought it better not to
muddle him; for it might prove a puzzling
point of view to French minds.

He wirelessed me again, remonstrating;
but I told him that Herr Fromach, acting
upon instructions, had previously left the
Bandol arrondissement (or district), where
he had been hiding while the Sanary district
was being searched, and had passed into the
Sanary district, before the route de Bandol
was closed, by the search parties.

All this I received by wireless, yesterday,
from another "mutual friend." And I made
it clear that now the news had leaked out

that Herr Fromach was certainly in the Sanary arrondissement, he must be got off to-night, or he would inevitably be captured, probably before morning. I explained that we might pretend to have a break-down in the engine-room, and this would account for our hanging about, off Sanary, if any official inquiry should be made. I had to repeat this, twice, before the strength of my reasoning was fully appreciated; and after that, I suggested that perhaps it would be safer to stop "sending" until I had either got my man away, or failed. I asked him first, though, about the landing on the Point, and the position of the Mill.

He replied that the Point Issol came down into the Mediterranean on the western side of the Sanary Bay (which, of course, I knew from the chart!), and that it "concluded" (which amused me) in a long, low snout of black rock, which could be boarded, as the night was calm, right at the point end, with a little scrambling. The Mill, he told me, lay right up on the brow of the Point.

He went on to remind me (as if I did not know!) that there was practically no tide in

the Mediterranean, as along the shores of
"Angleterre," and so I need make no "math-
ematics" of this—in which I agreed with
him!

After climbing upon the Point, I must go
up the "snout" until I came among the
trees, and here I would find a central road,
which would lead me right down into
Sanary. The rest, he must leave to me; but
if I gave any "vocal" signal, he would advise the croaking of a bullfrog, which is
sufficiently common not to attract undue attention.

I replied that Herr Fromach had already
arranged with me, to answer the howl of a
dog, three times repeated, for dogs, I understand, are plentiful among the farms on the
land side, and so this kind of signal will not
be noticeable.

＊　　＊　　＊　　＊

July 23.

We arrived off Sanary last night, at 11.15,
and I went below, into the engine-room to
interview Mister MacWhirr.

"Have you arranged that break-down,
Mac?" I asked him.

"Is it Mister Mac Whirr you're askin', or plain Mac Tullarg, the greaser, ow'r yonder?" he asked me. That's just the way of him, and we understand each other very well.

"*Mister* MacWhirr," I shouted, in a way that made the engine-room ring, "have you fixed up that——"

Mr. MacWhirr thrust out an oily hand at me.

"Whist! For all sakes, whist, mon!" he whispered. "Do ye want to tell all the stokehold what we've gotten planned!"

"That's better, Mac," I said. "If you're ready I am. We're off Sanary now, and you'd better hurry the break-down. What's it to be?"

"I'm thinking," whispered MacWhirr, over the back of his hand, "as yon bar-iron as I've leaned so casual like near by the valve guide of the low pressure 'll maybe shift with the vessel rollin' so heavy." (The vessel was as steady as a rock!) "An' the guide 'll sure get a wee bent. Oh, aye, we've a spare; but I'll no charrge it to the ship, Captain; for I'm not thinkin' as yon would be justice to Mr. Johnson, as is a fair man to work for, an' a countryman; though I'm not sayin' as he's not a wee inclined to meanness for a Scotsman.   But I'll no ha' yon on ma conscience.   If the guide's to go ashore to be straightened, then the cost must be shared by you an' me, Cap'n, in the proportion of oor shares o' the siller we make this night."

"That's all right, Mac," I said, laughing a little.   "Your conscience shall be kept pure and undefiled.   I'm going up on the bridge now, so get a move on with the accident."

I went up on to the bridge, and I had been there scarcely more than a minute when there was a muffled jar from the engine-room, and the screw stopped turning.   I'm pretty sure that Mac had throttled down handsomely, before he let the "rolling of the vessel" roll the bar-iron into the guides, so as to ensure the gentlest sort of "accident" possible.

I heard him now, shouting at the top of his voice, cursing and making the very kind of a hullabaloo that he would never have made had there been much the matter.

"Which of ye left yon bar-iron there?"

I heard him roaring. "I'd gie ma heid to
know; for I'd bash the man into hell an' oot
again, I wad that! . . . Mac, away doon,
an' tak' two of the men an' rouse out the
spare guide, an' get a move on ye. There's
two, an' maybe three, hours' work here for
us!"

I ran down off the bridge, and met Mac-
Whirr at the foot of the ladder.

"I'm feared ye'll ha' to anchor, Cap'n,"
he said, in a voice you could have heard fore
and aft. "There's yon fool greaser, though
he'll no own to it, made a store closet o' ma
engine-room, an' stood a two-inch bar of
mild steel on end, in a corner, like you might
in a fittin' shop ashore; an' the ship's juist
rolled it slam into the valve guide o' the low
pressure an' we'll ha' two, or maybe three,
hours' work to fit the spare. Heard ye ever
the like o' such damned aggravatingness,
Cap'n!"

I assured him that I hadn't, and ran forrard to put the anchor over.

Now, I had scarcely done this, and the
sound of our chain cable ceased echoing
across the quiet water, when there was a hail

out of the darkness, and a voice, speaking fair English, though with a strong French accent, asked—

"What vessel is that?"

"What the devil's that to do with you?" I asked. "Who are you, anyway?"

"I'm Lieutenant Brengae, of the Destroyer *Gaul*," said the voice. "You are not very civil, Captain, are you? It is the Captain, is it?"

"I apologise, Monsieur Brengae," I said, hurriedly. . . . (It was evident that there was a warship in the Bay itself!) "But Monsieur will understand that I am annoyed, when I explain that we have just had a break-down in our engine-room.

I could have fancied that I heard the Lieutenant, down in the darkness, stifle a vague exclamation. There followed a few moments of absolute silence, during which I ran over all sorts of possibilities in my mind. . . . All the probabilities and possibilities of his suspecting us of being there for any other reason than I had given. At last he spoke—

"I am sorry, Captain, to hear of your

misfortune," he said. Then with a charming air of friendliness, he went on: "Our second mechanician (engineer, you call him), Lieutenant Cagnes, is with me in the boat; we are enjoying a promenade. We will come aboard, Captain, if you will invite us, and have the pleasure of a talk. I will polish my poor English upon you; and my friend will be pleased to assist your mechanician, in any way he can. Lieutenant Cagnes never can resist the call of the machinery. It will be for him a pleasure most great to be of assistance. And for me, Captain, perhaps, if you weary of your own ship, you will come across to *La Gaul,* and split (is not that the idiom) a bottle of our friend Cassis with me?"

I did not hesitate an instant in my reply; for I had thought like lightning, as the Lieutenant was speaking, and it was plain that he had strong suspicions of the reality of our accident.

"Come aboard, Monsieur, by all means," I said. "Your offer is downright good *entente cordiale!* I daresay my chief engineer, Mr. MacWhirr, will pal on with your

friend; but for me, I fear I shall have to
decline with regrets; for I have certain letters which I must get off, at this opportunity. Perhaps, Monsieur would cause
them to be posted for me to-morrow."

My reasoning had shown me that it was
most necessary that they should see at once
that we were genuinely disabled; and I
could tell, by the change of tone in the
Lieutenant's voice, that he was half-way to
doubting he had any cause for seriously suspecting us. Also, by getting him to post
the letters, I hoped I should be able to get
rid of him early.

I had a ladder put over, and they came
aboard at once, and a couple of active young
men they seemed, too. I took them, myself,
down to the engine-room, and left them with
Mac, explaining that I was no engineer, so
could not explain the nature of the trouble;
but that doubtless Mister MacWhirr would
be able to give all particulars.

I smiled to myself. I could picture Mac-
Whirr giving them particulars in broad
Scots.

As I left, I heard Mac begin:

"I'd ha' ye to unnerstan', gentlemen, as that's noo engineers the like o' the Scottish in this worrld. I mind me when I wer' in the *Agyptian Queen,* runnin' fro' Belfast to Glasga———"

That was as far as I heard, before I reached the decks. I stopped there to laugh. Mac would certainly polish his *English* for him!

Then I went round the decks, to make sure there were no give-away things about. I found everything correct; for I had previously had the aerial wires, of my wireless installation, un-rigged; for a tramp steamer, under the circumstances, was better without the display of such luxuries.

Half an hour later, Jales (the steward) knocked at my cabin door.

"Them two Frenchies is going off in their boat, Sir," he told me. "One of 'em says as you wanted him to post some letters."

"Thank you, Jales," I said, raking my letters together. "I'll come up myself."

I found the two officers standing ready by the side ladder. They seemed to me almost apologetic in their manner, as if they were ashamed for having suspected me. It was obvious that my plan of allowing them to invite themselves aboard had produced exactly the effect I had hoped for. Moreover, as I had expected, half an hour of Mac's Scots version of the English language had proved sufficient to stunt both their desires for more exact information, either on the cause of our accident, or on the finer glazes that may be given to our English speech.

"Monsieur MacWheer has been very gracious," said Lieutenant Brengae. "But he will not allow my friend to *salir* his paws— is not that the idiom, Captain? So we will take your letters and return; for we have a slumber most great upon us."

"That's certainly a complaint that calls for hammock treatment, Messieurs les Lieutenants," I said. "Many thanks for offering to post my letters. Don't apologize for inviting yourselves aboard. I'm sure we're always open to give instruction in Scots English and engineering at any hour of the night. Mind the step!—as we have it in our idiom. Go-o-d-night!"

And I bowed them both down over the

side, in a somewhat puzzled state of mind, while one of the watch held a lantern over the ladder, to light them.

This showed their boat; and I could not help thinking it curious that two French lieutenants should go "promenading" with a fully manned gig of six oars, with each man of the crew armed. There is, of course, no accounting for tastes. But to me, it looked less like "promenading," than doing a sort of glorified sentry-go.

I stood and listened to the sounds of their oars die away into the distance across the bay; then I gave the word to lower the dingey, which we carry on davits across the stern. It is a light, convenient boat, and pulls well with two men.

I did not have the oars muffled; for I would not put myself into the position of allowing the men to suspect that I was mixed up in anything irregular; also, if we were discovered, prior to reaching the Point, there would be no material for evidence to prove that I was not also indulging in the favorite water "promenading" of the south coast. All I did to quiet the sounds of the oars was to tell the two men to "pull easy."

I took my night-glasses with me and studied the end of the long, low point on our port bow, which I knew, from its position, must be the Point Issol. It was a simply perfect night, so quiet that from some place, far in the bight of the Bay to the Eastward, I could hear the constant, interminable karr, karr, karr, of the bull-frogs, in some unseen marshland, ashore.

Presently we had come so close in that I could see the stark outline of the low snout of rock, black against the clear night sky to the westward.

"Gently! Gently!" I said to my men; and then, after a minute, " 'Vast pulling. Back starboard!" and the boat's gunnel was rubbing gently against the rocky end of the snout. I climbed out of the boat, and fumbled my way up on to the rock. Then I turned to the men.

"Lie off a couple of lengths," I said. "Don't smoke. Chew, if you want to, and keep your ears open for my hail."

"Aye, aye, Sir," they said, and I turned up the black slope of the Point.

I went slowly, for about ten fathoms, listening, as I went, and doing my best, for obvious reasons, not to stumble on the sharp edges of the rock surface. Then I stopped and adjusted my night-glasses and made as thorough an examination as possible, all round me.

So far as my glasses showed me, there was no kind of shrubbery or cover anywhere near—nothing but just the bare mass of the back of the long snout, in which the Point ended.

Farther up the slope, however, I could see the vague straggle of odd small trees, and above them, a squat tower showed, black and silent against the night. This, I presumed to be the Mill, near which I was to signal to Herr Fromach that I had come for him.

I put my glasses in my pocket, and continued slowly and carefully; but in spite of my care, I slipped twice, and the second time, I sent a small lump of rock rolling and clattering down the right-hand side of the Point. The "plunk" it made, as it entered the calm water, seemed to me to be loud enough to be heard half across the absolute silence of the Bay.

I stood for nearly a minute listening, but there was not a sound anywhere, and I knew that there was no reason, in the ordinary course of things, for me to trouble about the noise made by a smallish piece of rock tumbling into the water. But my state of mind was naturally a little tensed up by the situation.

I began to go upwards again towards the old Mill, and presently I had come among the first of the odd trees. They were small, and I could tell by their smell that they were pines.

Presently, I was quite close to the old Mill. It stood about twenty to thirty feet high, in a clear space, near the brow, to the right hand, where the Point sloped down into the Bay of Sanary. But ahead of me, I could see vaguely that the pine trees grew thicker, and seemed to cover most of the landward portion of the Point. To my left, the rock sloped away broadly into a small bay, and I could see numbers of stunted trees here and there, scattered oddly.

I literally tip-toed up to the side of the
Mill, and there I squatted low down,
silently, and stared round through my night-
glasses for maybe two or three minutes.
Once, I thought I saw something move
among the odd trees on the left-hand slope
of the Point; but after looking fixedly for a
time, I could not be sure I had seen anything.

I stood up then, and walked quietly round
the Mill; and after about a dozen steps, I
found that I had come. opposite an open
doorway, with a small pile of rubble just
tumbled loosely across the old threshold.
I had a sudden thought to step inside; but
a feeling of repugnance of the unknown possibilities of the old place, stopped me, and
I stood absolutely still again to listen.

It seemed to me that I never was in such
a silent part of the world; for, except for
the vague and monotonous karr, karr, karr
of the bullfrogs, somewhere in the bight
of the long bay, and the occasional far-off
howling of dogs ,among the hidden farms,
there seemed no other sound at all.

Then I heard a faint noise near me; that

made me listen the more intently. I could not locate it at first, and I drew back, out of a line with the dark, open doorway, and squatted down once more, so as to be hidden. Also, as any one knows, who has ever done any "night work," one can generally see objects better, the nearer the ground one gets.

I squatted still for quite a minute, and heard the slight noise twice. And then, as I looked up, I found the cause; for a length of broken wire was swinging gently, as an ocsional slight air of wind moved it. I could only see it when it swung idly, between me and the night sky.

I stood up noiselessly and reached for it. I had a sudden, vague, perhaps absurd, suspicion of a trap, in my mind, and I thought I would make sure the wire was no more than a broken end, swinging from the old structure. I caught the end, and gave it a good hard tug, and fortunate it was for me that the night was no darker, or I should not have seen in time to jump; for there was a vague rumble above me, and then I saw something revolve against the sky. I made one jump to the side, and as I did so, some heavy mass fell close to me, with a crash that seemed to echo through miles of the quiet night. I ran several steps, like a cat; then stopped and listened. But there was no sound anywhere, and I began to realize what an ass I had been; for I had pulled at some hanging bit of wire, which had probably been fixed at some time or other to some woodwork of the old Mill.

I walked quietly over to the fallen mass and felt it. I was right in my supposition; for I had simply pulled down a large portion of a rotten beam, and come very near to making my night's work thoroughly unprofitable in every sense of the word.

I guessed that I had better get done with my business, and be off. I held my wristwatch out in the starlight, and managed to see that it was just on the half-past twelve. As I did so, a clock, somewhere along the shore, struck the half-hour, and I raised my hands to my lips and howled three times like a dog. The sounds were most horribly mournful in that lonely sort of place, and I could almost have given myself the creeps, with the way that the last of the infernal

sounds seemed to die away and away, among
the black masses of the trees that lay all
along inland of where I stood.

I waited for about five minutes, listening;
but there came never an answer; and then
I howled once more, and I felt that if I had
to make the beastly noises again, I should
want twice the cash that was coming to me.
I had not thought a man could have made so
weird and horrible a cry, so infernally able
to disturb about ten miles of silent night.
I felt that half the people of Sanary would
be getting out of their beds, to stare up at
the black bulk of the Point Issol, to discover
the cause.

Yet, still there came no answer; and presently, after waiting a little longer, I thought
I would walk quietly a short distance from
the old Mill, along the inland portion of the
Point.

I went very carefully, looking round me,
every moment or two, and I found, after
about twenty or thirty steps, that I was in a
kind of gloomy little road, with the small
pine trees thick on each side of me, and the
night full of their rich, oily smell.

I stopped here, and looked down among the trees that covered the right-hand slope. As I did so, I was sure I heard a faint rustle to my left, and I whirled round, but there was nothing visible; nor could I hear anything.

Presently, I went a little further along the road, which had begun to lead down towards the hidden town. And all the time, as I went, I stared to right and left; for I was quite sure, on two separate occasions, that I had heard some further sound, almost as if something were following me among the trees; but on which side I could not be sure.

Abruptly, as I stared down the slope to my right, I saw distinctly a vague movement among the dark boles of the trees. I felt I was not mistaken, and I squatted down again near the ground, and stared. For quite five minutes I remained like this, and there was not a single noise, or movement of any kind, to suggest that there was any one near me. Then, as I stood upright, I saw something move again among the trees; and the suggestion came to me, like a flash, that I should

make quite sure it was not Herr Fromach
dodging me in turn, waiting for me to give
the signal again. So, without waiting a
moment, I just clapped my hands to my
mouth, and let out the first of the three
howls. As I did so, a most extraordinary
thing happened, I heard some one turn in
the path, not thirty yards before me, and begin to walk hurriedly away. I howled again,
and the walk became a run; and then, suddenly, there was a rush of feet, and a loud
crying in the night, about a hundred yards
away, and a sound of scuffling and muffled
cries and a fall and a voice shouting "Attrapé! Attrapé! Attrapé!"

There came a number of voices shouting,
and then a quick command, which was followed by a silence, in which I heard a man's
voice protesting monotonously.

There rang out, far and clear, three or
four notes on a bugle, and immediately the
whole night was filled with enormous beams
of light, that circled and poised and then
rested immovably along the length of the
Point. I saw the tops of the pine trees shine
like ten million fronds of silver against the

light; and down among the trunks of the trees on the right-hand slope, there burned great silent splashes of light.

Behind me, up on the highest brow of the Point, the old Mill stood like a chunk of white fire, every edging of broken stone or mortar picked out with the great blazes that beat in on every side; and in the light, standing immovable in a silent row, as if they were statues, was a long line of French manof-war's men, with rifles and fixed bayonets. They were drawn clean across the Point, the ends of the line vanishing among the trees on each side.

I comprehended thoroughly the perfectness of the trap into which I had walked. In some way, a complete knowledge of what I had sent by wireless, must have been obtained by the authorities. There were warships lying in the Bay, and it had been easy to arrange everything. The two lieutenants, probably with a score of other officers and boats, had patrolled the mouth of the Bay, and kept a watch for every vessel that came "near in." They had come aboard, apparently in casual friendly fashion; and when they had left, they had evidently been confirmed in their own minds, that my ship was the one they were looking for. Possibly, the whole of the Point Issol had been silently invested, in readiness, for some hours, and every step of my way, even up the "snout," and my little adventure with the old beam, must all have had their silent onlookers.

A rare bit of drama I had been providing the fleet with! And there had obviously been orders not to interfere with me in any way; but to give every chance to the German to meet me; for it was not me they wanted, but the German, Herr Fromach, with (as I had already guessed) the almost priceless plans of the new additions to the great Fortress of Toulon.

As I stared, fascinated, at the line of silent man-of-war's men, with the blaze making their bayonets shine like spikes of fire, some one touched my shoulder, gently, and I whirled round.

Monsieur Brengae was standing close to me, saying something, which I did not hear; for over his shoulder, down the slope, among

the trees, there were vaguely seen move-
ments of hundreds of men among the
shadows.

"Monsieur, the Captain has come ashore
for a promenade?" I realised that the Lieutenant was saying, in the most courteous
fashion possible.

"Good Lord!" I said, staring. "That you,
Monsieur? . . . What are your men
doing? Is it an execution?"

"The men!" he said, looking at me, in
a mild kind of way. "But what is Monsieur's
remark? What men shall he mean?"

"Why!" I said, and turned up the brow
towards the old Mill. But there was not a
man visible, of all the silent guards who had
stood a moment before across the breadth
of the Point, between me and the sea.

I laughed, as I looked at the Lieutenant.
Evidently they were acknowledging nothing
unusual, except a searchlight display.

"Remarkably fine show!" I said, staring
down at Lieutenant Brengae.

"A little welcome, shall we say?" said the
Lieutenant, smiling; but his lips came back a
bit too much from his teeth, and quite spoilt

the friendly tone of his preceding words.

"Perhaps, Monsieur, the Captain had an assignation," he said, still in his gentle way. " . . . No?"

"Certainly not, Monsieur," I answered.

"Ah!" he said, smiling still; but now the way his lips left his teeth was almost a sneer. "Perhaps Monsieur came ashore to sample the cheese of the country, or maybe it was a foreign cheese . . . perhaps Monsieur has a fondness for cheese, shall we say, Roquefort? But I fear the shops are shut tonight!"

"I'm not much of a French scholar, but I knew enough to remember that *fromage* goes for cheese, and that the little Lieutenant was rotting me; he was simply punning on the German's name. But I only laughed, as good naturedly as I could, in the circumstances.

"I fear Monsieur disbelieves me?" I said.

"Perhaps as the shops have closed up," said the Lieutenant, looking at me fixedly, "Monsieur the Captain will not want to buy any cheese to-night?"

I thought of the scuffle I had heard, and it

was plain that he was telling me that Herr Fromach had been caught.

"Promotion, Monsieur Lieutenant, is a glory for the young man," I said. "I perceive that Monsieur is in the cheese business, and hopes to make a profit!"

He stared at me, half fierce as he wrestled dumbly to shred out my exact meaning. Then he shrugged his shoulders; but was still at a loss how to get even with me for the way in which I had levelled him up, in his own little word-game of quiet cut-and-thrust.

However, I saw no reason for giving him time to mature a reply, and raising my cap, I said *Bon-soir*, and turned seawards.

Lieutenant Brengae accompanied me to the end of the snout of rock, and stood silently by me, while I whistled for my boat.

As I got in, he murmured: "Good-night, Monsieur the Captain. I have cheesed it for you, is not that the idiom?"

This was evidently a great and successful effort, and he threw his chest out, with a queer little swaggering motion.

I laughed quietly, as I answered him—

"Perhaps, in the circumstances, Monsieur, I must accept your idiom as correct," I said. "Good-night, Monsieur le Lieutenant."

"Good-night, Monsieur the Captain," he said. And so we parted.

When I got aboard, Mac had everything ready, and I up anchor and away, at once, as any one can imagine.

The searchlights of the warships followed me, as if in a silent unison of jeers at my night's imbroglio, until the Point la Cride hid me.

*   *   *   *

July 28.

I went ashore to-day at Gib, where I posted the following letter to my friend, Lieutenant Brengae, of the Destroyer *Gaul*—

"MY DEAR LIEUTENANT,

"I felt at our last brief meeting it would have been out of place to attempt to force upon you the truth that I did not go ashore on the Point Issol to meet the German, Herr Fromach. It was not, in any way, a fitting moment to insist upon the truth of my statement. .But the time has come when I must do so, in the hope that you will now, of your natural courtesy, accord me belief in my word, which I fear you were once inclined to discredit.

"I did not go ashore on the Point Issol to meet the German; for at the moment that I went ashore, my Second Mate, in one of our life-boats, was embarking Herr Fromach in the Bay of Bandol, some miles away. My little excursion to the Point Issol was planned solely to direct attention to that one spot; and my wireless messages (of a cypher too easy to be secret!) were purely bogus; for I myself sent both my queries and my replies; repeating them courteously, until I felt sure that the warships in the Bay of Sanary could not have failed to assimilate them. Need I explain more! Except that I landed Herr Fromach at Algeciras, not more than two hours ago.

"I have often wondered who was the innocent and unfortunate visitor you 'captured' on the Point that night, He must have been almost as bewildered as you were later, when you discovered that, after all, your investment in, shall we say, Roquefort, on the Point Issol failed to prove a profitable speculation!

"I trust you will admire the smartness of my little plot, in the same courteous spirit in which you and the Admiralty genially assisted me to carry it out.

"Believe me, dear Lieutenant Brengae,
    "Yours faithfully,
        "G. GAULT—
            "*Master.*

"P.S.—There is just something more I must add, in closing. I do not believe in spying, and, incidentally, I've no particular use for Germans.

"Further, I'm an Englishman; and as this war between Germany and France (our friend) seems now to be a certainty, I think that you will be pleased to hear that Herr Fromach went ashore minus his plans. When he comes to open the envelope which contained them, he will find some really first-class blank paper.

"I was offered five hundred pounds to pick up the respected Herr and land him safely in Algeciras. I accepted the contract, and have fulfilled it faithfully; for it is my fixed principle always to carry out any engagement I undertake. As I have said, I landed him two hours ago in Algeciras, and my commission is honestly earned.

"The plans, however, are another matter. And, to go into details, they are, at this moment of writing, *en route* to the Governor of Toulon, in a registered package, with my compliments. Let us shake hands, my dear Lieutenant. As you would yourself phrase it, in excellent idiom: 'I have Herr Fromach on buttered toast.' In England we should not, perhaps, be so particular about the butter; we should account just plain, dry toast sufficient.

"Shake hands, old man.

"G. GAULT."

CHAPTER X

THE ADVENTURE OF THE GARTER

s.s. *Edric,*
January 17.

I'M back passenger carrying, and I suppose I'm a bit of a fool; but there's a certain young lady aboard, who's managed to twist me round her finger more than I should have imagined possible a few days ago, when we left Southampton.

She's next to me at the head of my table, and we've rather cottoned on to each other. Indeed, I'll admit I like her that well, I've broken my general rule, never to allow a passenger up on the lower bridge; for she's been up there with me several times lately, and I feel a bit of an ass; for I guess my officers are sure to be poking fun at my expense, among themselves. A ship's Captain should keep his lady friendships ashore, if he hopes to have things run smooth aboard.

She's a dainty little woman, with pretty hands and feet, and heaps of brown hair. Looks about twenty-two; but I'm old enough to know she's probably about thirty. She's too wise for twenty-two. Knows when to keep quiet; and that's a thing twenty-two is generally too bubbly, or too much of a know-all, as the case may be, to have learnt.

"Captain Gault," she said to me this morning, after we had walked the lower bridge for the better part of two hours, "what's in this little house here, you're always going into?"

"That's my chart-room, Miss Malbrey," I said. "It's where I do most of my nautical work."

"Won't you take me in and show me?" she asked, in a pretty way she has. She hesitated a moment; then she said, a little awkwardly: "There's something I want to talk to you about, Captain Gault. I simply must go somewhere where I can talk to you."

"Well," I replied, "if I can be of any service, I shall be downright pleased. Come along in and look at my working den; and talk as much as you like."

I guess that shows she can wrap me round her finger, more than is good for me; for I've made it a rule for years, to keep my chart-room strictly private and strictly for ship's work. At least, I mean I've tried to!

But there you are! That's what happens to the best of us, when a lass takes our fancy. They get us on our soft side, and we're like tabbies round a milk saucer. As MacGelt, an old engineer of mine, used to say: "It's pairfec'ly reedic'lous; but I canna say nay to a wumman, once she's set me wantin' to gi'e her a bit hug." And there you have the Philosophy of the Ages in a nutshell! At least some of it.

Now see how things came about. We'd no more than got inside the chart-room, than Miss Malbrey asked me to close the door.

"Please turn your back a moment, Captain, will you? I sha'n't be a minute," she said.

The next thing I knew, she called out to me that I could look round. And when I did so, she was shaking her skirt down straight with her right hand, and holding out to me something in her left which I saw at once was a garter, of surprisingly substantial make.

"Take it, Captain," she said, looking up at me, and blushing a little. "I'm going to beg you to do me a very great favor indeed. See! Feel it. Do you feel those cut-out places inside, and the hard things in them? . . . Surely, Captain, you know what it is."

"Yes," I said, rather soberly. "I know what it is, Miss Malbrey. It's simply a jewel-runner's garter. I'm sorry. I don't like to think of a woman like you doing this sort of thing——"

She waved her hand to me to stop.

"Listen a moment!" she said. "Do listen, Captain Gault. This is to be my very last trip with the sparklers. I've made up my mind to drop it, for good. And I should never have troubled you about it, only there's one of the Treasury spies aboard, and she's spotted me; and I shall simply be caught; and oh, I don't know what to do, if you won't help me, Captain Gault. You're so clever at running the stuff through.

You've never been caught. I've heard lots of times about you, and the way the Customs never can catch you with the goods. Won't—won't you, just this one time, to save me from being caught, run this through for me? And I promise you it will be for the last time. I shall never try to run stuff in again. I've made enough to live on quietly; and now I guess I want to be shut of it all. Will you help me, Captain Gault? Promise me you will?"

What else could I do? I promised, and now I'm booked to run this pretty little lady's stuff through, willy-nilly; and never a thought does she seem to have that I may get caught, and suffer fine and maybe imprisonment. But I certainly don't mean to get "catched," if I know anything about it!

"Where are you going to hide it, Captain? Do trust me," she said.

"I never show my pet hiding-places to any one," I told her. "You see, my dear young lady, if ever you have to keep a secret, keep it to yourself; that's my rule. If I told first one person and then another, where I hide some of the trifles I sometimes

take ashore duty-free in New York, why I
guess I should be in bad trouble pretty
soon."

"But I'm a trustable sort of person, aren't
I, Captain Gault?" she assured me. "And
I *can* keep secrets. Why, if I couldn't, I'd
never have put anything over on the
U.S.A. Treasury. I've never once been
caught and it's only through an accident
that I've become suspected. But I don't
care. I'm tired of it; and I'm going to stop,
really and truly, and be good and settle
down. Now do be a dear man, and let me
be *the* privileged one person in the world,
and let me see your famous hiding-place
that all the Customs officers are sure exists;
but which they can never find. Now do,
Captain."

"Miss Malbrey," I said, "a man's but a
poor, weak thing, in the hands of a pretty
woman; if you will forgive an honest com-
pliment——"

"Gee!" she interrupted, laughing right
away down in the back of her eyes. "I'll
forgive you anything, Cap'n, pretty near,
that is, if you'll make me the only other

person in the world who knows the truth of the great mystery."

"Well," I said, "you'll have to give me your solemn word you'll keep it a secret till the end of your life."

"Sure, Captain Gault. I'll die on the rack first," she told me, twinkling at my seriousness. "Now be a good man and show me. I declare I'm all on the quiver with wondering where it is. Is it down in the hold, or where?"

"Miss Malbrey," I said, slowly, "you're sitting within six feet of a human miracle of a hiding place.

"What? Where, now?" she asked, staring round and round, in a way that she surely knew was disturbingly taking to a plain sailor-man.

"See," I answered. "You shall open it yourself. You see that the thin, steel beams over your head are not cased with wood, as they are in the cabins and saloons. They're just plain, small, solid steel T-girders, with no size about them, you would say, to hide anything—eh?"

"Well now," I continued, "look at the

'beam' just above your head, and count the square-headed bolts that go through the flange on the forrard side of the beam, up into the deck that makes the roof of the house. Stand on this chair. I will steady you. Now! The seventh bolt-head. Take it between your finger and thumb and see if you can turn it to your left. . . . Can you?"

"Yes," she said, with a little gasp of effort. "Just a teeny, weeny bit. . . . But nothing's happened!" she added in a disappointed voice.

"Ah, believe me, dear lady, that's just the beauty of this little hiding-place," I said. "If a Customs searcher happened on that bolt-head and twisted it a little, as you have done, he would merely suppose that it was a loose bolt, because nothing would happen to make him think otherwise. But let me help you off the chair. Now come along to the other end of the beam. See, I twist the second bolt-head here, close to the side, and now I can lift out a bit of the steel flange here, right in the center of the beam, with a row of false bolt-heads attached.

Look! Do you see the hollow in the deck planks which the flange covers? There's room there to hide a hundred thousand dollars' worth of pearls or stones.

"Now, do you realise the cunning of it all? Before this bit of removable steel flange can be shifted, even a hundredth part of an inch, the seventh bolt on the starboard side has to be turned to the left; then one has to go across to port, and turn the second, from the side of the house, to the right. Then one has to come here to the center of the beam, and catch hold of the twenty-fourth bolt from the starboard side, and the twenty-ninth from the port side, and pull outwards, evenly, and there you are. When it's closed, it is almost microscopically invisible. I tell you, Miss Malbrey, the man who thought out that dodge, and had the old beam taken away, and that doctored one fitted in place of it, was a smart chap, and no mistake!"

"And that man was you, sure enough Captain Gault," she said, laughing, with her pert little head turned on one side, and clapping her two small hands.

"You flatter me, my dear lady!" I answered her; and refused to tell her whether I was the one who'd had the beams altered, or not. All the same, the notion is a smart one; and I pride myself on it; which is certainly one way of letting the cat out of the bag!

"Ah! Well, Captain Gault, you're sure one smart man!" she told me, when she had helped me hide the "smuggler's garter" in the recess above the beam flange. "I'd never have thought of a notion like that. I guess I'd better run away now, and take Toby for a run, before you get tired of me. Isn't he a darling dearum now. Kiss me, pet!"

This, perhaps, it may be as well to explain, was not a direct invitation to me; but was addressed to her pet dog, Toby; a toy pom, which had gotten quite friendly with me; but I've no use for it. I abominate lap dogs; but I've not said so to the young woman!

"Miss Malbrey," I said, "I'm getting quite jealous of the dog!"

And by this speech, you may gather that

I had slightly lost my head. I can't, say I've quite got it back, even at this present moment of writing. She's a confoundedly taking young woman!

January 18.

Mr. Allan Jarvis, the Chief Steward, came up to see me this morning. He's a man I trust; which is more than I do most people. We both hail from the same town, and when we're alone together, we drop the Mr. Jarvis and the Captain Gault. It's just plain Jarvis and Gault, as it should be, between men who are friends and have helped one another put through more than an odd deal that had money at the bottom of it.

"Look here, Gault," he said, as he lit one of my cigars, "you're going some strong with the young lady in Number 4 cabin."

"You don't say, old man," I replied. "Well?"

"It's just this," he told me. "Don't trust her too much. I've a notion she's playing a game with you, that's got more than an odd kiss or two at the bottom. Look at this, before you start to cuss me for butting in!"

He handed me across a folded newspaper-clipping, headed—

"AMERICA OPENS A NEW PROFESSION
FOR WOMEN.

"The Treasury Recruits Twelve Pretty Women to play I-spy-I on the Transatlantic Jewel Runners."

"Well!" I said, "What of it. You're not going to suggest to me that Miss Malbrey's one of them——"

"Open the thing, man!" he interrupted. "Unfold it!"

I was doing so, as he spoke, and now I saw what he meant. There, on the cutting, was a half-tone photo block of a pretty girl, looking at me, and the girl was most extraordinarily like Miss Malbrey (Alicia Malbrey, she's told me is her name).

"It's not her, Jarvis, man," I said. "I'll not believe it. I just won't believe that sort of thing of her. Why, man, look at the face; the eyes are too close for her, and this is a younger woman altogether. And, besides, it's impossible. Why, she's just the opposite to anything of this kind. Why, she's a——"

I pulled up short, for I had nearly told Jarvis that she was as much of a smuggler, in a small way, as either he or I.

I pondered a moment, whether I might not tell him; but before I could decide, he chipped in again—

"Poor old chap!" he said. "You sure got it bad!" And that shut me up.

"Have it your own way," I told him. "But I happen to have a special reason for *knowing* that the little lady's all right."

"Ah!" he said, getting up, "I know the special reason well enough, Gault. We all feel that way, when we're a bit gone on some woman. The worst of it is, they've generally too much brutal sense, not to use our little feelings to their own advantage! Ha! Ha! old man! I love to quote your own vinegar sayings against yourself!"

And with that, he left me, taking his beastly cutting with him. All the same, I've had some pretty fierce thinks; but I've decided the *evidence* is quite insufficient to condemn my dainty lady of the laughing eyes. Oh, Lord, haven't I gone and got it properly!

January 19.

"Don't you just love my doggie, Captain Gault," said Miss Alicia Malbrey, to me this afternoon.

"Well," I answered, "I suppose, Miss Malbrey, there's all sorts of ways of looking at things."

"Now you're sure just dodging me, Captain, and I won't have it!" she told me. "You do love my Toby boykins, don't you? Tell me honest true."

"No, Miss Malbrey," I replied. "If you want an honest answer, I do not like Toby or any other kind of a lap-dog. To my mind a dog is an unsuitable object for a woman's arms; and a woman who kisses and nurses a dog, cannot, it seems to me, prize herself as highly as she should, or she would shrink from such physical intimacies with what is, after all, simply a stunted little animal, less useful than a cow and less courageous than a common rat!"

"Captain Gault," she rapped back at me, "you're sure forgetting yourself. Let me tell *you,* a dog's as good as a man, any day!"

"There's no accounting for tastes, Miss Malbrey," I said, smiling a bit. "We men do not hug and kiss our dogs. We consider a woman pleasanter and more suitable."

"I should think so!" she interrupted. "Do you mean to say you'd compare a woman with a dog, Captain Gault?"

"That's just what I refused to do," I said. "You see, dear lady, you began by asking me, did I like lap-dogs—or something to that effect; and now, because I like to think they are inferior to women, you're belaboring me and pretending that I've been saying just the opposite! Oh, woman! Woman! In our hours of ease——! Now, if, instead of asking me what I thought of your lap-dog, you'd asked me what I thought of you —why then, lady of the winsome face, methinks I would have never ended the nice things I could have said. Why, of all the dainty-faced——"

I paused, to hunt round for words to describe further, without offending.

"Yes, Captain Gault?" she prompted.

I looked at her. There was not a sign of anger now in her face; only a sort of *waiting*

—I could almost have thought it was a kind of triumphant expectancy.

"Yes?" she said again, scarcely breathing the word.

I looked at her in the eyes, and suddenly I realized that I was being allowed to look right down into them; and a woman only does that, when she is either luring or loving.

Was she flirting with me, or did she really care? I put it to the test, and caught her up in my arms and kissed her full on the lips.

"Oh!" she said, with a gasp.

A minute later, she laughed, breathlessly.

"I knew you'd not be able to hold out against me much longer!" she said.

She laughed again, in her quaint, pretty way.

"Now, shut your eyes a moment, Captain, dear, and see what love will bring you!" she said; and brushed my eyes gently shut with her small hands.

There was a rustle of skirts; the rattle of the bells on Toby's collar; a faint creaking, and then a dainty, mocking laugh—

"That's as much as is good for you for one day, Captain Gault," came her voice; and I opened my eyes just in time to see her closing the door.

New York,
January 20.

My Chief Officer came along to my cabin this morning, after I had interviewed the officer of the Customs. My cabin had just been searched; and I had declared all that I meant to declare!

"I don't know if this concerns you, Sir," he said; "but it seems as if it might. The breeze blew it out of one of the Customs men's hands, and I put my foot on it before they saw where it had got to. I thought you'd better see it at once."

"It does concern me, very much indeed, Mr. Graham," I said, grimly, as I read the crumpled note he had handed me.

"Treacherous little devil!" I heard him mutter, under his breath; and I knew that he also guessed who had written the note. It was fairly brief and brutal, and quite comprehensive—

"Look in the Captain's chart-room. Middle beam. Turn seventh bolt, from starboard side, to left; and second bolt, from port side, to right. Then catch hold of the twenty-fourth bolt, from starboard side, and twenty-ninth, from port side, near the middle of the beam, and pull out sideways. A part of the flange will slide out; and there is a recess cut in the deck planks above. The diamonds are there in a 'garter.' Remember, I am not to be mentioned in the case at all. He's a slippery customer; but I guess I've got him nailed down solid this time.—No. 7. F."

"Perhaps there's time yet, Sir, to go one better than her," said my Chief Officer aloud. "They'll have to go back to her for fresh instructions, now they've lost this paper. Can't you get up to the chart-room and nobble the stuff, before they get there. You may be in time, yet. Heave the blessed stuff over the side, rather than let them do you in, Sir. That's what I'd do!"

I looked at him. I daresay he thought I

was a little dazed. I fancy I shook my head; for this was as bad as my worst suspicions could have suggested it. In that moment, I was thinking far less of the "trap" the Customs had prepared so carefully for me, than of the completeness of the ruin of my faith in women in general.

"Mr. Graham," I said, "a man's a preposterous ass if he hasn't learnt to mistrust any woman, by the time he's thirty!"

"Yes, Sir," he answered, seriously enough. "Unless she's his mother."

"Ah, just so!" I said. "Unless she's his mother. But they can't all be our mothers; confound it! I'll get up to my chart-room. No, don't come, Mr. Graham. It's too late now to undo what's been done. . . . The treachery of it! My God! The cold, brutish treachery of it!"

I reached the chart-room, and peeped in through the after window. The Customs were already in the place; four men were in there. And, suddenly I heard Miss Malbrey's voice. I could see her now, over by the starboard side, with her back to me. She was directing operations, as cold-bloodedly as you please. Evidently, they had sent for her, now they had lost her note, to explain how to work the secret catches in the steel beam.

"No," I heard her say. "The seventh bolt from the starboard side. Twist it to the left. That's right. Yes. The second from the port side—— To the right. Now, Mace, the twenty-fourth from the starboard and twenty-ninth from the port. Do get a move on you. I don't want the Captain to catch me here. Pull——"

I opened the door, and stepped inside.

"Sorry if I'm a little premature, Miss Malbrey," I said. "May I ask what you are doing in my chart-room?"

I held the door open for her to pass out. But she took no notice of me; only, the cheek and ear that I could see were a burning red. I was grimly pleased that she felt some sort of shame for herself.

"I must ask you to leave my chart-room, Miss Malbrey," I said quietly. "This part of the ship is not open to passengers."

"Aw! Quit it, Cap'n!" said the man she had called Mace, who was standing on my chart-table, lugging clumsily at the bolt-heads. "We got you at last, I guess, Cap'n; an' you don't come any of that tall stuff over us. . . . Is these two the right ones, Miss?" he finished, looking over his shoulder at Miss Malbrey.

"Yes," she said, not much above a whisper. "Pull out parallel with the deck, evenly——"

"It's coming," said the man. "We sha'n't be long now, Cap'n, before we has you just where we been wantin' you this two years, an' more!"

I said nothing; but walked across to my telephone, and rang up the Chief Stewardess.

"Please come up to my chart-room at once, Miss Allan," I said. "Bring a couple of stewardesses with you."

I hung up the receiver, just as the man on the table worked the sliding portion of the flange clear of its sockets. He put up his forefinger, and raked along the recess in the deck-planking above, which he had laid bare. He was obviously disappointed, and made it clear to every one.

"Aw!" he said. "Watcher givin' us, Miss! This is sure a bum do! There's nothin'! Just plain nothin' at all!"

"Quit talking foolish!" said Miss Malbrey, in a voice sharp enough to show the kind of metal she was. She made one jump to a chair, and then on to my chart-table. She pushed the man, named Mace, to one side. . . .

"It's gone!" she called out, suddenly, a moment later, in a voice that was half a scream. "It *was* there! . . . A proper runner's garter. There were five thousand dollars' worth of stones!"

She whirled round on me.

"You wicked man!" she called out, in a thorough little fury. "You thief! You thief! What have you done with my stones. . . ."

"Ssh!" said one of the other search officers. "There's some one coming. They're the Captain's goods we are looking for, Miss. Don't you worry yourself, and talk rash. You mind how you saw Cap'n Gault hide some di'monds; an' you done your duty, like a proper citizen, an' told us."

In a way it was almost laughable, if it had not been for the way the pretty little woman was showing the poor, bad stuff she was built of. It was plain enough to me that the man was prompting her, and trying to steady her down to normal control again, before she gave away more completely the plot they had made to trap me.

But he could not quiet Miss Alicia Malbrey, disgruntled feminine Treasury spy, in that moment of complete failure of all her hours and days of treacherous planning. And then, in the midst of her wild storming at me, as she stood there on the table, the chart-room door opened, and in came the Chief Stewardess, with two strapping looking stewardesses behind her.

"Ah, Miss Allan," I said. "Perhaps you would kindly see Miss Malbrey to the passengers' part of the ship. I've tried to explain to her that she is intruding here; but I find that she does not quite comprehend."

"Aw! Quit the tall talk, Cap'n!" growled the man called Mace, in an ugly sort of way. "An' you other leddies, let the young leddy be. It's just more'n *you* dare do,

Cap'n, to shove in between our lot, an' what we got to do!"

"Indeed," I said, as gently as a father. "Am I to understand that Miss Malbrey is a Treasury official?"

The man, Mace, hesitated and turned red. He had evidently let his tongue off on the gallop, ahead of instructions. While he paused, just that one moment, one of the other search officers chipped in.

"Go ahead, Cap'n," he said. "You gotter do what you think proper. Only don't try interferin' with us men. I guess the young lady's not one of ours."

He gave Mace a nudge to keep quiet, and I saw that Miss Malbrey was not to "come out into the open" as a full-blown Treasury spy; for then her value, as such, would be enormously lowered. In other vessels, she is evidently to continue her unpleasing profession.

I smiled, with a good deal of bitterness in my heart. Then I nodded to the Chief Stewardess, who went up to Miss Malbrey.

"Come now, Madam," she said, quietly. Let me help you down." Then in a lower voice, I heard her say: "Don't make a scene, Miss Malbrey, for your own sake. Come now, be a wise young lady. You shall come to my own cabin, and tell me all about it."

I smiled again; this time at the genuine humor of the thing. The Chief Steward-ess's tact seemed blended with more than a possible curiosity; but I certainly admired the tact—the result of years of the tradition that "scenes" and passengers must be kept out of sight of each other.

Miss Alicia Malbrey went quietly enough. It seemed incredible that I had held her in my arms, within the last twenty-four hours, and that she had kissed me, freely, and apparently with some pleasure in the process. I began to doubt the sex of Judas!

As she went past me, I had a strong im-pression that she would never tell the real facts to the Chief Stewardess, or any one else, for that matter. Even such women as Miss Alicia Malbrey have a way of prefer-ring that people should not credit them in full with the treachery that ripples so naturally and smoothly through their systems.

And, fortunately for me, it had all led to nothing; for kind Nature has blessed me with a certain caution and foresight, and an ability to abide by some of the teachings of Commonsense and Experience. One of these teachings is: Never use two heads to keep one secret! The hiding-place above the beam is one I have long since given up; and I removed the "garter" of stones, within half an hour of putting it there; and later, I placed it in another, and even more cutely conceived hiding-place, where it lies at this present moment.

January 27.

By methods of my own, I discovered the address of Miss Alicia Malbrey. And I took a taxi there this morning to have an interview with her, which pride, prejudice, and a number of other things demanded.

I was shown into a pretty sitting-room, and told that Miss Malbrey (though that was not the name given!) would see me in a few minutes.

When, at last, she came in, she stopped

in the doorway. She was carrying her pet dog; and she looked pale, and I could almost have imagined, a little frightened.

"What—do you want, Captain Gault?" she asked, in a low voice.

"Won't you sit down, Miss Malbrey," I said. "You must not feel worried. I am not here to bully you."

"I—I'm not afraid of you, Captain Gault!" she said, with a little nervous hesitation.

She came across the room, and sank into a small chair.

"What is it you want of me?" she asked again. She was still white and nervous.

"I've come to return you some property of yours, or the government's," I said.

And, with the word, I stooped forward over her, and unbuckled Toby's collar. Taking it by the end, I tore it open lengthways.

"Hold your hand," I said; and I poured a little cascade of diamonds into her palms.

"Oh!" she cried out; and stared at me with very wide opened eyes.

"Do you remember the last day aboard, when you missed Toby's collar?" I asked.

"Well, I had borrowed it from the little brute. The Chief Steward gave it you back, later. He told you it had been found on the saloon floor. Well, while I had the collar, I 'loaded' it with your stones. I was practically sure, by then, that you were a Treasury spy; but I kept hoping against hope, that you would find it impossible to 'sell' me, when it came to the point. I felt that your womanhood would make that impossible to you. We men have some queer, silly notions, haven't we? No, I'm not going to bully you. I promised you that. Besides, it's not my way."

She had gone a deep burning red of shame. Then the red sank out of her face; and she was whiter than ever.

"But," she said, in a very low voice, staring at me strangely, "if you knew what I was, Captain, why did you do this? Why didn't you keep these stones, as—as spoils of war?" she held out her hand, and stared from me to the diamonds.

"They were not mine," I said. "And I smuggled them ashore for you, just to keep my promise to you—a sort of joke. You see, as I was practically sure you were a Treasury spy, I knew your dog would not be a likely 'suspect.' It is one of my little prides, that I always keep a promise."

"What a strange, strange man you are!" she said, almost under her breath.

I stood up.

"I'll say good-bye now," I said.

At the door, I heard her cry out something in a low, queer voice; but I never looked back. Faith dies hard with me; but it stays dead, when it does die.

In the street, I got into my taxi and drove off. In my hand, I still held the ripped-up dog's collar. I rattled the two brass bells and smiled. Then I unscrewed each of the bells, and took out the pea from each. They were big peas, covered with a celluloid skin. I peeled off the skins, and there I held in my hand two magnificent ten-thousand dollar a-piece pearls.

You see, I had made one stone kill two birds, or rather one dog collar carry two lots of smuggled jewelry.

Rather neat, I call it. Look at it every way you like, it was neat—eh?

www.ingramcontent.com/pod-product-compliance
Lightning Source LLC
Chambersburg PA
CBHW020440270626
47155CB00022B/670